A
HARLEQUIN
Book

HIS SERENE
MISS SMITH

by
ESSIE SUMMERS

HARLEQUIN BOOKS
WINNIPEG ● **CANADA**

First published in 1966 by Mills & Boon Limited,
50 Grafton Way, Fitzroy Square, London, England.

© Essie Summers 1966

Harlequin Canadian edition published March, 1967
Harlequin U.S. edition published June, 1967

Printed in Canada

1093

CHAPTER ONE

THE operator said: "This is a person-to-person call from Auckland by Mr. William Durbridge to his secretary, Miss Smith. Is Miss Smith available, please?"

I said: "Miss Smith speaking. Go ahead now, please."

The call didn't come through immediately. It gave me time to predict how Mr. William would start the conversation. It was easy ... he would say: "Is that Miss Smith? ... My *Serene* Miss Smith," and I would experience the familiar, indeed inevitable, desire to scream. To say something quite unpredictable, to answer anything but serenely, anything, something to knock him off his supercilious perch, to take that mocking note out of his voice.

But I wouldn't, of course. I wouldn't give him the satisfaction of that. I would remain completely imperturbable. I'd kept it up for over six months now. It had become a habit.

His voice came through quite undistorted by the thousand odd miles of land and ocean between us, with that disturbing timbre that did things to me and, as always when speaking to me, faintly ironical.

When he had uttered that derisive formula he went on, "And how are you this morning, dear Miss Smith? No, no, don't tell me, I don't need to ask. You're neat, white-collared ... your desk is tidy, you're poised at the ready with a ball-point in your immaculate hand, not a hair out of place, a spare ball-point beside you. You are, aren't you, Miss Smith? Please don't spoil my image of you by telling me you're not."

Just as well Mr. William couldn't see me gritting my teeth. I said calmly, even primly, as one might humour a child who was showing off, or a boss in whom one had no personal interest, "Yes, Mr. William, everything is under control. Now ... ?"

He coughed in an affected way. "You really mean: 'Now, come to the point, Mr. William! Don't waste the bawbees uttering polite nothings on the phone. Keep the costs down . . . even in a firm like Durbridge's.' How my grandmamma will approve of you when at last she gets back from the States!"

I made my tone as suave as his. "I sincerely hope so, Mr. William. You know my views about that."

"I certainly do. You'd prefer the real head of the firm to be a man, not a woman. Though I find that quite a paradox. In your neat little circumscribed existence you haven't much time for men, have you?"

I allowed irony to creep into my tone. "Oh, I've no objection to *working* for them, Mr. William." I coughed, said: "What did you want, Mr. William?"

His voice changed immediately. "I want you to send some flowers for me, Miss Smith."

I saw my knuckles tighten on my ball-point and instantly made them relax again. What did it matter to me? Mr. William regularly sent flowers to Veronica Boleyn. Everything of the most exotic and most expensive.

I said automatically: "Any particular time you wish them to arrive?" (If it was for a corsage for her to wear at some function he was escorting her to when he flew home, it must be timed perfectly.)

"I want them sent express . . . by taxi."

I frowned. "Then they'll have to send them to the studio if they're to reach her immediately. No use sending them to an empty flat."

There was a maddening chuckle. "Miss Smith, you're leaping to conclusions—how out of character! These are not for Miss Boleyn, they're for Bunty."

Bunty! Who on earth was Bunty? And how stupid of him to suppose I would know her.

I said, "Oh," with very little expression, then, quickly, "What message would you like on the card, Mr. William?"

"I've got it written down, Miss Smith. I'll read it slowly and you can read it back to me. Here goes: 'How could you do such a thing when I'm a thousand miles from you? I've telegraphed Doctor Robertshaw to instal a nurse immediately. Flying home tomorrow. All my love, pet, Bill.' "

Pet! How idiotic.

I read it back in a dead flat tone. I must allow no hint of surprise to creep into it. Where did this Bunty come into Mr. William's scheme of things? Only last week he'd been positively dancing attendance on Miss Veronica Boleyn . . . sending her flowers, buying her nylons, dating her. He—I clamped down on all the questions clamouring in my mind and said firmly: "You won't want this sent from Florista's, I suppose? Should I try the Garden Grotto?"

His voice carried sheer amazement. "Why not Florista's? That's where I run an account."

I swallowed, sought for words, but didn't find them. If that—that idiot of an employer of mine didn't know, I wouldn't tell him! How could I, anyway? I couldn't say: "Have you forgotten that that girl at Florista knows Veronica Boleyn intimately? That she won't be able to resist telling her you're sending flowers—*and* loving messages—to some other girl!"

Serve him right if Veronica treated him to a scene when he got back.

I couldn't think of a thing to say in excuse for my query, so said as if I'd not heard, "Yes, Mr. Durbridge, of course. Now, what address?"

"Address? My home address, of course. She's not in hospital . . . was that what you thought? I wouldn't allow her to go to hospital. She injured her leg quite badly. Fell off her horse."

My thoughts were whirling. He must think I knew all about this Bunty. Might do him good to realise I didn't . . . that I did not take the same keen interest in his affairs that presumably he thought all his staff did. She must have been staying on the family estate at Tattoo Bluff. Hm. That meant that this affair was serious.

I pulled myself up and said: "Yes, Mr. William. I'm sorry, but when you said you'd have them sent out by taxi I didn't dream you meant away out past Waitati."

His voice softened. "I wouldn't do this for anyone

but Bunty. But I can't get home today. It's quite impossible. But I'll get the first plane down tomorrow, though I have to stop off in Christchurch. I meant to have a day there, but now the chap I'm going to see is going to come out to the airport to conduct business there and I'll get the next flight. Now, Miss Smith, I want the flowers in a bowl . . . a really choice arrangement. Tell them to spare no expense but they must be garden type flowers, no hothouse ones. There must be lavender and mignonette and those tiny sweetheart roses and . . . let me see . . . maidenhair fern and stocks and cinnamon pinks. But nothing exotic, mind."

"Yes, Mr. William, I'll attend to it immediately. Do you wish for a car to meet you at the airport? Very well, I'll see to it. If you give me the number of your flight from Christchurch I'll check time of arrival. Is there anything else, Mr. William? No? It was a very busy day yesterday in the shop. Most satisfactory."

"Good . . . and by the way, Miss Smith, you might be interested to know that I sat next to your former employer at the Master Drapers' dinner last night."

I was careful not to sound dismayed, only interested. "Oh, Mrs. Reedway. How was she?"

"I found her most interesting. Quite a warhorse, isn't she? But she told me I was a fortunate man to have secured your services as a secretary. And I wouldn't imagine she was given to undeserved praise. But of course I can understand it . . . *you* would never put a foot wrong, would you, Miss Smith? It wouldn't be easy to find a fault in an automaton."

He chuckled most infuriatingly.

Never put a foot wrong! If only he knew! Evidently Mrs. Reedway, praise be, had kept her own counsel.

The dry voice continued : "No comment? How wise . . . when in doubt say nowt! I also met her charming son, Lance Reedway. He was on my other side. Women were in short supply. Quite a lad, isn't he?"

I didn't want the taunt of "No comment?" again, so I said hastily, "Yes, quite a lad. Rather spoiled, of course. Mr. William, was there anything else?"

"Not a thing, Miss Smith. Good morning."

The moment he hung up I realised with dismay I hadn't asked Bunty's proper name. Well, it was his own fault ... if he'd kept strictly to business instead of being sarcastic at my expense, he'd not have talked himself out of giving it to me. I rang the exchange and asked to be reconnected, but there was delay on the line and by the time I got his hotel he'd gone out.

Now I was in a fix. I could hardly ask members of the staff if they knew the name of Mr. William's latest fancy! That wasn't the sort of thing he would expect from his confidential secretary.

I had an inspiration. I could ring Doctor Robertshaw, though I'd be lucky if I got him in. A country doctor could be twenty miles away.

Luck was with me. I phrased my request carefully.

"Doctor Robertshaw? It's Mr. William Durbridge's secretary here. He rang me from Auckland to ask me to send flowers to someone at Tattoo Bluff and in discussing—er—certain other business matters forgot to tell me her name. She's had an accident, out riding, and he mentioned he was getting you to engage a nurse for her. Could you tell me her name? He only said Bunty ... a nickname, evidently."

He sounded the typical country doctor, bluff, friendly, warm-voiced. "Yes, he's never called her anything but Bunty—but the name is Miss Pamela Huntingdon."

I thanked him and rang off.

What a beautiful name ... Pamela Huntingdon. Not like Serena Smith.

And it wasn't a *new* girl-friend ... *he's always called her Bunty*. And he didn't want orchids or begonias for her, but garden flowers ... lavender ... mignonette ... sweetheart roses ... cinnamon pinks. My knuckles were white again. Then this *was* serious.

But in that case why had he been rushing Veronica Boleyn off her feet these last few weeks? Veronica, who was as provocative as Anne Boleyn had been, four centuries ago. I told myself it was just as well I had said no to all Mr. William's invitations when first I came to work with him. He was about as faithful a suitor as Henry the Eighth!

If this Bunty had always been in his life had they quarrelled? If so, when? Before he asked me out? Or had Bunty always been in the background while he trifled with other girls' affections? Or was that coming it a little strong? There was probably nothing of affection in his feeling for Veronica. And it was just possible, I supposed, that he had classed me, at first, with Veronica's type. Someone he could take out, then drop. Perhaps he was given to sudden infatuations.

All the time my boss had been running her round I'd known a strong stab of regret at intervals, regretting my firm refusal the first time he'd asked me to lunch; and the second even firmer one ... no, let's be honest, the second one had been a curt refusal. And the next time I'd asked him please to stop bothering me, that it was most embarrassing for a girl to keep refusing the man whom in all other things she was bound to obey.

But now ... no need to regret. It wouldn't have led to anything. Not if I had read aright the love and concern in his voice just now. It was possible, of course, that he had asked me out just after he had quarrelled with Bunty, out of pique. Then, failing me, he'd seen in Veronica the ideal antidote when first she had dawned on his horizon.

Oddly, I'd always thought of his affair with Veronica as nothing but infatuation. But Bunty ... that was another kettle of fish. Bunty, whom he thought of not by her own lovely name of Pamela but by a nickname, intimate and dear. Not an orchids and begonia person but one with whom he associated sweetheart roses! Someone whose place in his life was wholesome and abiding.

I shook myself mentally. Snap out of it, my girl. You'd vowed never again to get your private life tangled up with your boss's. It didn't pay. And while at present Mr. William Durbridge was running Durbridge's, in no time his reputedly formidable grandmamma would be back. Probably even more of a dragon than Lance Reedway's mother! Get on with your work, Serena, and stop speculating!

The flowers first. I dialled Florista's number.

Veronica Boleyn's friend did answer the phone. That fact, plus the note of surprise in her voice when I said it was to be addressed to Miss Pamela Huntingdon, Tattoo Bluff, Blueskin Bay, confirmed my opinion that Veronica knew nothing of any Bunty. Or Pamela.

When I said, finally, that it was to go by taxi, her voice positively squealed as she repeated, "By taxi? That'll cost the earth!"

I regret to admit that it gave me the greatest satisfaction to be able to say reprovingly : "Those are Mr. Durbridge's instructions. When it comes to Miss Huntingdon he spares no expense."

It was just as well it was a busy day. I threw myself into work. I must not lose my hard-earned reputation for speed and efficiency.

Things went well the next morning till five minutes before the junior accountant was to take Mr. William's Chevrolet out to the airport. His mother-in-law rang to say his wife was departing for the nursing home and Greg Harper simply took off.

The manager came into me. "Serena, you'll have to go for the Chief. I'm not trusting that Chev to any of the young lads who'd love to be behind that wheel. And any of my older, more reliable ones can't be spared from their departments. We're phenomenally busy. And you're used to driving a Chev."

Mr. Jennings always called me Serena when there was nobody about. He was Father's Session Clerk and always in and out of the Manse.

I burst out laughing. "Mr. Jennings, you're not honestly comparing Dad's Old Faithful with that slick model of Mr. William's?"

"They all come from the same kennel, Serena, and their working parts are in the same place—though do remember there will be more power under your foot than when you drive Angus's. Don't waste time, there's a good girl. Just get weaving. I should think you'd like a couple of hours off . . . it's a sparkler of a day."

I couldn't really think of any valid reason for refusing. He handed me a bunch of keys. I went into the outer office, explained where I was going—to envious remarks, of course—and went along to the staff cloak-room. I couldn't help but be glad that although this pinafore frock was neat garb for the office, it had a loose swinging jacket that I often wore over it outside the business, that transformed it into a really smart street suit. It had a plaited leather girdle that was most unusual and the millinery department had made me a hat with a leather tassel on it that matched perfectly. I very hurriedly bought some new long gloves down at the counter and a new bag to which I transferred all the oddments from my old one.

I justified this to myself by saying that it was very necessary to dress well for a business appointment with one's chief. After all, as a draper, he expected his staff to dress well.

I offered up a silent prayer as I slid behind the opu-lent wheel that I would arrive at Momona with every gleaming enamelled inch unscratched.

I manoeuvred it out from the staff and customers' cars in the parking lot and headed up Great King Street, then turned right into St. Andrew's Street and cut across George Street to get out of the busy Dunedin traffic. I'd hit the Main South Road from Lookout Point.

My truant imagination veered towards thinking how nice this would have been had it meant anything. If I'd been Mr. William's wife, for instance, picking him up . . . if there had been no Veronica . . . no Bunty!

Anyway, I told myself savagely, with a man as fickle as he was, it was just as well I'd stuck to my resolve never again to be involved with a member of the management of any firm I should work for. It would have been far more humiliating to be made a fuss of by one's boss for a few weeks and then have to go on working for him when suddenly he fancied someone else or . . . made it up with his first love !

No, you just had to keep your business life and your private life separate.

It was a glorious New Zealand day of early autumn. The time when Otago—like Scotland—was at its best.

The Taieri Plain lay below the main highway, patch-worked with green and gold and dotted with the white of countless sheep. The silver ribbon of the Taieri River threaded through on its way to the sea. The gorse on the hillsides was dazzlingly yellow and its nutty frag-rance came in at the open window. The sky was blind-ingly blue with never a cloud.

One of the charms of Dunedin was that in a few moments you could be outside the city limits, with lagoon and shore, gorge and native bush to delight your eye. And I loved its sober pace of life after bust-ling Auckland.

Not that Auckland hadn't a charm of its own with its hundred bays and semi-tropical lushness, with its bathing from September till Easter, but generations of Scots forebears made me love this ... a grey, spired, university city that sometimes knew the magic and the hush of newly fallen snow, the flame of rowan berries, forest plantations of larch and spruce and pine. Of course Father said that in Dunedin his foot was on his native heath. He had gone to theological college here and had always longed for a Dunedin parish. And Mother? She was a North Islander, but she simply loved anywhere where Dad was happy in his work.

I struck off the main road and out on the new high-way to the airport tucked between the Maungatuas and the coastal hills. I had five minutes to spare.

What views Mr. William would have on a day like this ... the sheltering curve of the Peninsula Hills about the harbour; White Island and Green Island flecking the sea out towards the lilac horizon beyond which waited Antarctica; the ranges of Central Otago hills that led back to the Southern Alps ... he would see the twelve thousand feet of Mount Cook rearing up from them, see the rivers cleaving the gorges on their impatient gallop to the Pacific.

Sunlight struck on silver wings. There she was ... the Friendship, coming down. A most unaccustomed nervousness gripped my throat. Like most New Zealanders, because of the country being divided into two main islands, I'd done a lot of air-travel. How horrible it would be if the landing gear went wrong, if a cross-wind suddenly ripped across the tarmac, if a tyre exploded on touching down ... Suddenly I realised that the Friendship *was* down and running towards the Terminal.

He was almost last off, coming along, despatch case in hand, bare-headed as usual, the sun glinting on the short-cropped brown hair, so broad you didn't at first realise he had height to match till he towered over you.

I watched a woman of about thirty run right to the barrier and be caught up in someone's arms, eager, unembarrassed. I envied her fiercely.

I stood by the row of pastel-coloured easy chairs, saw Mr. William's eyes cast about in search, naturally, of one of the male staff members. He said to his companion, "Well, cheerio, Josh, drop in at the office before you go back. Nice to have seen you."

The next moment his eyes widened in surprise. "Why, Miss Smith, fancy you being here to meet me! Or stay ... are you meeting someone else, in your dinner-hour?"

I shook my head. "No, Mr. Harper was coming, but his mother-in-law rang him to say his wife was going into the nursing home just as he was leaving to collect you, so Mr. Jennings suggested I should come." I permitted myself a slight smile. "My father has a chev ... about a dozen models before yours ... and he decided that qualified me to be trusted with yours."

"Oh, I expect he knew you'd drive as circumspectly as you do everything else, Miss Smith, with no desire to speed or take risks."

I once more experienced a desire to scream. All this repression wasn't good for me.

"Have you your luggage to collect, Mr. William?"

"Yes, wait here, I'll get it."

"No, I'll come through with you, Mr. William. They've taken the luggage through and the car's just across from there."

"Yes, I know, but we'll have lunch here in the cafeteria—less crowded and decidedly more pleasant than in town. I've a spare set of keys, thanks." He looked back over his shoulder as he made off, mischief in the sherry-brown eyes. "At last I get my own way . . . I lunch you and you can't do one thing about it."

I couldn't. I waited, trying to cultivate an air of supreme indifference.

During the first course Mr. William kept to the topics one would expect from a chief after a few days away. But just as we started our chicken and potato salad, he said abruptly : "I had a long yarn with Lance Reedway after I phoned you. I found it very interesting."

I knew the colour had come up in my cheeks, but I addressed myself to slicing the meat off a leg and managed to say lightly, "I expect you would find it interesting. Reedway's is similar to Durbridge's in every way, privately owned, about the same size, and run by a woman in trust for her descendants."

He laughed outright. "How pat you have it, my dear Miss Smith . . . all neatly docketed and filed away in one of the pockets of your mind. However, you've slipped in your analysis. That was not the reason for my interest. Another roll?"

I took one, broke it, said quickly, "What a perfect day you must have had for flying. You'd see Mount Cook and Mount Tasman perfectly, I imagine?"

"Yes. *Was* Mrs. Reedway the reason you were rather dismayed when you found out after I engaged you that my grandmother is the real owner of Durbridge's, not me?"

Bother the man !

But he had to be answered. "Oh, yes. I decided when I came down here that I'd prefer to work for a man." For the first time that day I looked directly and frankly at my employer. "One can't have everything, I know, but I would also have preferred an older man, a married man."

He leaned back in his chair, regarded me quizzically and said : "Well, well, just a little more human today, aren't we? May I ask why?"

I shrugged, still clinging to my reputed serenity. "People are always watching a single man and his secretary. I find it embarrassing. It interferes with the efficiency of the office. I enjoy my work and don't welcome distraction."

"Have you always felt that way? Do you really enjoy keeping the different compartments of your life sewn up into watertight pockets?"

I took time to answer that. Then : "Yes. It means I can give my mind fully to my job."

"Does it work?"

"It has so far, yes."

Mr. William finished his chicken, put his plate to one side, leaned his elbows on the table and regarded me too closely for comfort. "But only while you've been with us, I suggest . . . six short months?"

"I don't know what you mean, Mr. Durbridge."

He grinned. "Young Reedway and I didn't talk about drapery management. We compared notes . . . on you."

I put my knife and fork down, swallowed what I had in my mouth and said : "Did you have to? I mean, didn't my reference tell you all you needed to know?"

"All I needed to know to engage you. Not all I *wanted* to know. I found out all sorts of intriguing things. Your real reason for leaving, for instance."

I looked at him steadily. I was not going to look guilty.

"Mr. William, that sounds as if you think I lied. That I came here under false pretences. My reference stated that I left Reedways of my own accord . . . well, I did. It also mentioned that I wished for a position down south, to be with my family when Dad was shifted down here. I did wish that."

His lips were twitching. "Come, come, Miss Smith. You know perfectly well that I would never doubt your word. How could I? You're a model of integrity, a paragon. But Lance Reedway told me you really left because he was getting serious about you."

"Serious? Mr. William, Lance Reedway has never been serious about anyone in his life. In fact he's had so many girls I doubt if any woman would take him seriously. And his mamma watches him like a hawk. Possibly one shouldn't blame her—a very eligible son and quite a likeable one, heir to goodness knows how much. She won't want to see him married for his money."

"So you didn't take him seriously?"

"I've just said. No one would. I've seen so many of his affairs simply fizzle out. There's no real harm in Lance, but no depth either. I couldn't imagine him anything but a draper ... pleasant to the public, a lot of facile charm, but nothing to him."

"No? Could be you've been mistaken, Miss Smith, incredible though that seems. I think there is more to him—now."

My voice went squeaky with surprise. "You mean you felt *that*? On so slight an acquaintance?"

"Well, his mother told me he's been taking some subjects at university. Arts."

"*Arts* subjects? Lance?"

His voice was amused, "And all due to you, Mrs. Reedway vows."

"Due to *me*? How could—oh!"

Mr. Durbridge said: "Ah, the penny's dropped." I knew I'd gone a painful red.

He added: "You've remembered your parting shot to Mrs. Reedway!"

I couldn't speak for the moment and he added: "At last my Serene Miss Smith has lost her maddening serenity. Don't bother to regain it, Serena, I like you better this way."

I said, chokingly, "Did you *have* to discuss me that way? Surely I've given you satisfaction in my work. Doesn't it suit you to have an efficient but *impersonal* secretary?"

His eyes became serious. "I like a more friendly atmosphere about me, really. Efficient, yes, but as cold as a clay pipe! So naturally I asked Lance Reedway if you'd always been like that. He was astounded, said: 'Serena Smith? The stormy petrel of the office. Good lord, I've known her for years. She's got the worst flair for unorthodox adventure that I've ever known ... and the warmest heart.' I can tell you, Miss Smith, I stared. I thought can this possibly be my walking iceberg of a secretary, with whom I scarcely dare venture on a joke?

"So thus encouraged, your Lance Reedway opened out." My employer chuckled again. "I could see it all ... his mother catching him kissing you in the reserves and—"

"Just a moment, Mr. Durbridge," my voice was icy calm. "You have it all wrong. He was *trying* to kiss me. There *is* a difference. Had Maude Reedway appeared one second later she would have seen me smacking her precious son's face. But she arrived just too soon and positively stormed at me. She seemed to think I'd made an excuse to get up in the reserves with Lance.

"I lost my temper. Yes, Mr. William, I do have a temper. I let fly, and as always happens, said too much. It was when she hinted—no, more than hinted, it was really an accusation—that I was deliberately encouraging him because he was such a catch that I really saw red. She had turned to Lance and said : 'As for you, you've no discrimination ... can't you see the girls only see you as the inheritor of Reedway's?' "

"And you said?" prompted Mr. William as I paused.

I looked at him, sighed, said : "I think you know what I said. That stupid Lance seems to have told you all."

"Actually Lance didn't go quite as far. It was Maude Reedway who told me."

I was flummoxed. "*Mrs.* Reedway did?"

He nodded. I could have shaken him. He was enjoying this. "Yes, she said you retorted : 'Why, I'd never dream of marrying anyone like Lance ... not if he owned a dozen drapery shops in his own right. He can't hold a candle to any of the impecunious divinity students I meet in my father's house by the dozen ! Men who stand on their own feet, who put themselves through varsity and theological college. Men who've got brains, not just salesmanship.' And then you gave in your notice."

At that moment the waitress appeared with our sweets so we waited to resume till she was out of ear-shot.

I said in a low voice, rather unhappily, "Mr. William, I've been ashamed of that ever since. Dad was awfully disappointed in me. He said that was intellectual snobbery which was the worst form of all. But you know how it is when you lose your temper. I was so flaming mad to think Mrs. Reedway thought I'd chase her son that I just went in boots and all."

Mr. William leaned back on his chair and gave way to mirth. "I'd love to have seen you! You've been so prim and proper that I was glad to know you really could act like that. And, Serena, that was mighty provoking of Mrs. Reedway. She admits it herself. But there again, evidently she'd had so much experience of seeing girls set traps for Lance that one could excuse her too. Miss Smith, don't snort. It's anything but serene and ladylike. And Mrs. Reedway thinks you've really done something for her Lancelot."

A silence fell. Then he said, in a quite different tone, "And it did something for me too." I looked at him inquiringly. "Well, I rather smarted under your refusal to come out to lunch with me. But now I know it was just a sort of reflex mechanism after such an experience, I've been given fresh hope."

I stared at him. "You've been given fresh hope? Mr. William, you must be—" I cut it off. After all, he *was* my boss.

He still grinned. "Go on, Serena. Say it . . . you don't need to keep up this Serene Miss Smith farce any longer. Don't have any inhibitions. Finish what you were going to say . . . well, if you won't, I'll do it for you. You were going to say: 'Mr. Williams, you must be mad!' But why, Serena, why mad?"

I looked at him soberly. "Can't you guess, Mr. William?"

He considered it. "You mean you're thinking of making it a permanent policy not to accept invitations from your employers? But I'm not exactly Lance Reedway's type, you know, nor do I let my grandmother—old autocrat though she is—rule my life. And I don't pursue the girls at the shop. I've never taken out another employee in my life."

I couldn't help a contemptuous curl to my lip.

"Not from the shop, oh no, Mr. William. But I've no desire to take my place in the queue along with Veronica and Bunty. I've never gone in for casual affairs and I certainly don't intend to start one with my boss."

His eyes glinted for just a moment, but he wasn't the sort to give himself away too quickly.

"Veronica? I can explain Veronica . . . if I need to. After all, I only took Veronica out after you turned me down, Miss Smith. But Bunty—" He stopped, and I felt I'd had about as much of his nonsense as I could stand. I pushed back my empty coffee cup and my chair and rose.

I interrupted him. "But Bunty you can't explain. I didn't think you could. Bunty sounds *nice*. Too nice to be hurt by me, or you. A girl who loves lavender and mignonette and sweetheart roses must be nice. My policy stands, Mr. William. And if you'd prefer me to seek another position, well, I will. I'd like a nice steady job with a family-minded sort of employer, with no alarms and excursions and no personal touches. The sort of job I could forget about as soon as I closed the door behind me at night." And I swept off towards the exit, leaving Mr. William to pay and follow.

CHAPTER TWO

HE didn't catch me up till I was opening the car. I hated the amusement in his voice as he said : "Go round to the other side, Miss Smith, *I'm* driving." His hand came over mine on the handle and took it away.

I said nothing, merely walked round to the other side and got in when he slid across and unlocked the catch.

He slipped suavely into small talk as we headed back to town. Talk of the shop, his buying expeditions in Auckland, the weather, the traffic on the road, and comments on the condition of the paddocks and stock that seemed extremely knowledgeable for a draper.

I replied as naturally as I could, but was aware of a tumult of emotion within me. Could I get back to being his Serene Miss Smith? I must try. I couldn't face terminating another job after so short a time. Not even one year.

Gradually the ordinary give and take of conversation soothed me, though I knew relief when we left the country for the suburbs and the suburbs for the city. Back in the shop things were bound to get away from the too-personal.

We turned up Great King Street. Not long now. One block and we'd turn into the firm's parking lot. He didn't slow down.

The next moment I was saying, "Mr. William, you've gone past."

He grinned. "Yes, purposely. We're having most of the afternoon off."

I felt immediate alarm. "Mr. William—"

"I'm going out to see Bunty, of course. You're coming with me."

I tried to sound calm. "Just drop me off here, Mr. William, and I'll walk back to the staff entrance. You don't need me."

"I've decided I do need you. And your time is mine, remember. Now do sit back and relax, Miss Smith. Don't be tiresome. Most employees would jump at the chance of a few hours off. You've had a week without your Chief's distracting presence and with your brand of efficiency I don't doubt everything is more than up to date."

"But I don't see why—"

"No, but I do. Now that's all there is to be said about it. Don't be tiresome, as I told you before. You're making too much of it. We'll be back at the shop at four-thirty. You can put in an hour's work and go home at your usual time." He gave his maddening chuckle. "You'll work better then. You certainly wouldn't now. Your blood sugar must be high."

I lapsed into silence. We turned over the overhead

bridge and headed up Pine Hill to the motorway. Given other circumstances I could have enjoyed it. Last winter I'd seen this under snow and it had been a purely Canadian scene with larch and spruce and pine plantations crowning these lovely hills.

At the end of the motorway lay the sea, a deep cobalt blue, and we swept down to Waitati.

"Blueskin Bay," said Mr. William, with the note of supreme satisfaction that people keep for the one spot on earth they love best.

I said, "Don't you find it inconveniently far out?"

He glanced at me and away again. "It's the only thing that really reconciles me to the shop life, having Tattoo Bluff to come home to."

I was completely surprised, in fact jolted. I stared at him. "Why, Mr. William! I thought you were almost obsessed by the shop—that you thought, breathed, lived Durbridge's."

"At the risk of sounding smug I'll say it just happens that I believe in throwing oneself into what one must do ... you know : 'Do with thy might what thy hand finds to do.' That's all. But Tattoo Bluff is *my* kind of life."

"Then why?"

"Because my grandmother wanted me in the business."

I was silent. Rather hypocritical then for him to have said when he was disparaging Lance Reedway: "But I don't let my grandmother, old autocrat though she is, run *my* life."

But I wouldn't pass comment. I was trying to get back to impersonal relations with my chief.

The road skirted the lagoon. I was glad we had no more conversation for a few miles. We turned off to the right when the main road went up Mount Kilmog, and began to climb a little ourselves, with Warrington Beach below us.

I heard a chuckle beside me and Mr. William's audacious voice. "You know, sitting in dignified and elevated silence really does something for a girl. You have a most exquisite profile!"

I turned in a flash, spoiling it, and before I'd time to restrain myself, heard my voice saying: "And of course you are a connoisseur in such things!"

Another chuckle, with a note of pure mischief in it. "I am. Just wait till you see Bunty!" When I didn't reply he added: "You know, if you were a blonde you'd really be something."

I started to say something and checked myself. I mustn't.

Foiled, he added: "But it's really a change to have a girl with nice, natural mouse-coloured hair she doesn't dye!"

I couldn't help it. I said sarcastically :"Does that mean that Bunty too is a blonde?"

He'd know by that "too" I meant Veronica.

"Well, she used to be blonde, but you know how it is, Miss Smith ... one day blonde, the next a gorgeous redhead. At the moment Bunty's hair is what I think the hair-stylists would call silver-gilt."

For a stupid, irrational moment disappointment washed over me. Silver-gilt hair didn't tie in with sweetheart roses and lavender. Silver-gilt sounded like mink and orchids. And it would have been nice to have thought, since one had no intention of allowing oneself to fall in love with Mr. William, that a man of his type *could* fall in love—and *had*—with a perfectly nice, wholesome type of girl.

"Not making any comment, Miss Smith?" asked that exasperating voice beside me.

"It doesn't need any comment—from me." I let my eyes wander to the Pacific below us, where the blue swept to the lilac horizon with just one small fishing-boat, seemingly motionless, in all its vastness. "This scenery holds one almost spellbound. A pity to be just ... er ... bickering instead of drinking it in, don't you think?"

He let a note of admiration creep into his voice. "You ought to be a diplomat's secretary, Miss Smith. I've never heard such a clever way of telling a chap to shut up. And you have a horrible knack of being right. Let's just enjoy it in silence. They say silence is easy, between kindred spirits."

He waited, for a bite I presumed, then said, "Sorry . . . I shall now hold my tongue."

But my racing thoughts came between me and the sheer enjoyment the scenery should have engendered.

"If you were a blonde," he had said.

I suppose he wouldn't have believed me had I retorted : "But I *am* a blonde!" I was. What Dad called a Scandinavian blonde, a throwback to that Viking ancestor who'd settled in the Orkneys, centuries before, on Dad's mother's side. It was because that colouring *had* made me "really something" that I had had it dyed mouse.

But nobody down here suspected it was dyed because blondes just don't dye their hair nondescript !

My looks hadn't brought me any happiness. I knew they had created a situation that ought never to have arisen in our family, our warm-hearted, closely knit family.

Once closely knit.

Pain, none the less stabbing because it was remembered pain, surged over me.

I could hear Patsy's voice again, with the hint of heartbreak in it, speaking to her best friend.

They had no idea I was in the toolshed.

"I'm so glad the family are leaving Auckland, Geraldine, and that because there isn't a post-primary unit attached to teachers' college down there they can't insist that I move with them. It will be heaven to be just me, Patsy Smith, not Serena's plain little sister. Who knows, I might even, given a decent chance, get a boy-friend who won't default the moment I take him home and he meets Serena.

"Taking it all round, Geraldine, I don't think I'm too unattractive, it's only that nobody can hold a candle to Serena. If she did it on purpose I'd hate her, but she doesn't. Serena is so darned nice. But she's always been bewitching. I believe even at kindergarten the boys fell over each other to carry her bag home.

"If she was selfish and spoiled or untidy and inefficient or *something*, perhaps the attraction wouldn't last, but she's just as nice inside as outside. Look at the way she gave up her varsity career when Dad had that illness. She took a secretarial training at nights and worked in a shop through the day till she qualified—and has never once hinted I'm the lucky one. And I'm doing exactly what she first set out to do. I'll even be teaching her subjects—history, English, geography. Oh, it's a mess!

"But it's a godsend Daddy has got a call to this church right down in the deep South. An answer to prayer. I'll stay up here, take an Auckland High School next year and make my own life, my own circle of friends. I even tried to hate Serena when Mark fell for her, but I couldn't. She was so horribly distressed. She certainly carved him up when he asked if he could take her out. I think she thought if she was scathing enough that he might come back to me . . . as if I'd want to be a second-best . . . but I'll stay up here, and Gerry, for goodness' sake invite me to your Whangaparoa beach-house for the holidays. I don't even want to go to Dunedin for Christmas!"

The bitterness of it was with me still. There was nothing I could do about it. And it had come so soon after that scene with Maude Reedway. It made me so mad, made me feel like a *femme fatale*. And I'm not. Not inside. It made me distrustful, of myself, I mean. I felt people, especially men, like me only—or mainly—for my looks. And what sort of guarantee is that for a woman's future? If illness or disfigurement came along, how would she hold a man's love? Take Mother, for instance. Feature by feature she's not beautiful at all. But something shines out of her, and everyone thinks she is, especially Father.

Everything rubbed it in, especially the short stories and novels I read. It was almost unbelievable how many of them were about the *plain* sister, the *plain* cousin! None of those stories ever showed a glimmer of sympathy or understanding for the too-pretty one, of the way her looks could mess up *her* life and make havoc of *her* relationships.

Not only with men, either, but with her business life too. I believed now I'd been happier behind the counter than anywhere else. I'd been just one of the herd then, because there had been five of us in the cosmetic counter, all picked for our looks. One was a flashing Spanish-eyed type of brunette, one a copper-top, and three of us were blondes. How thrilled I had been when I got my first office appointment, and more thrilled when my advancement to secretary had been so rapid. Till other girls had hinted it was not on my merits alone.

Then man trouble started. Or should I call it woman trouble? Lloyd Fanton had been such a pet, and all of forty-five. He'd been so embarrassed when he had given me notice, but had been very frank. "I'd never have thought Eleanor could turn jealous. It's just damn silly. Of course I'd had Miss Harmsworth for years. A real plain Jane. I'll have to look round for another of the same sort. But I made it plain to Eleanor that I was going to give you as long as you wanted to get yourself another job, that although I'd tell you you had to go, you must be allowed to give me the notice. I didn't want to put on your reference that I'd given you the sack."

It had been sweet of him, but it had rankled just the same. What was worse was that it had taken away my confidence. Little wonder that, after the flare-up with Maude Reedway and the conversation I'd overheard of Patsy's, I had arrived in Dunedin with mouse-coloured hair, and that I kept to sombre office garb and became prim and proper.

But seemingly it hadn't stopped Mr. William. He'd asked me to lunch with him the second week I'd been there. No doubt, I thought, mentally curling a lip, it was just a case of his being used to girls falling for him and his male pride was piqued. He had a nerve bringing me out here with him like this. Serve him jolly well right if this Bunty was mad with him about it. I could just imagine her ... probably was a crack rider, even if she had taken a toss. I suddenly felt very nostalgic for that country parish of Dad's way up in the

Bay of Islands, where we had had a pony of our own, where family life had been so uncomplicated.

But I had hopes that Patsy's wound was healing. She'd missed home horribly and to my parents' great delight had, after all, applied for and secured a Dunedin post in February this year. She had raised her brows over my mousy hair (I'd had it done in Christchurch on the way here) but had accepted my explanation that I was tired of bosses' wives and mothers looking at me askance because I was a dangerous blonde, ". . . and everyone thinks my natural colour is a dye, anyway, so what odds?" I'd grinned, seeing Patsy looked satisfied, and added : "And what a relief not to have other girls asking what colour my hairdresser uses and then being offended when I say it's natural!"

Patsy had laughed and said : "Serena, you've never been in love, have you? You'd really rather go on with a career, wouldn't you?"

I'd nodded. "True. I'd like to be married some day . . . but never quite yet. I'd like to experience a bit of life first, travel, broaden my outlook."

But now I couldn't help but look forward to seeing Moko Hills. I'd been told that area was a dream of a place. They always held the staff picnics there. The naturalists' club often came out here for field days. It was covered with native bush—which, of course, means forest stands, in New Zealand. The tree-planting association got self-sown seedlings from the forest floor for various beautifying projects and it was always being photographed.

The Durbridges had been early settlers here and from the very start had preserved a good area of bush, only burning off what they had needed for pasture. Some of the trees were said to be five or six hundred years old.

"There it is," said Mr. William, breaking our long silence. There was pride as well as affection in his voice . . . as well there might be.

It was a magnificent stand of bush, impossible to see

completely; some of it was tucked into the folds and gullies of the hills. It ran up over the crests and disappeared into other valleys far away. The trees had the bluish green of a tattooed warrior's skin that was so typical of Blueskin Bay. No wonder they called it Moko Hills. Moko means tattooed. On the next hill stood the homestead, built on the shoulder so it didn't lose the sun all day, with terraced gardens ablaze with colour spilling down the homesteading to the road where magnificent gates stood wide open.

It was much more on the grand style than I had expected. There was even a coachman's house, a stone one, at the gates.

"No coachman now," said Mr. William. "We put in cattle-stops to save opening gates every time. I turned the coachman's house into a museum. We dig up a lot of Maori artifacts round here, you know, and there were so many treasures people wanted to see up at the old house, so we brought them down and have special days. An old chap who is past working on the estate now sees to it. He and his wife have three rooms at the back. It gives them an interest. We have a lot of whaling station relics too. That was how this estate was first started. The original New Zealand Durbridge was brought out by the famous Johnnie Jones of Waikouaiti, who had a whaling station there. That was pre-church-settlement days, of course."

I said, "Oh, I must tell Debbie . . . my small sister, just twelve. She's absolutely mad on digging for Maori artifacts and so on."

Mr. William said : "Oh, good. You must bring her out here some time and I'll show you both round."

I said quickly, "Oh, no, we mustn't impose on your good nature. I'll bring Debbie out on the regular sightseeing days."

He laughed and let it go. As if I would! Just imagine the enmity I'd incur from this Bunty, who was possibly . . . just possibly . . . my employer's future wife !

The avenue up to the house was all English trees, hawthorn, chestnut, poplar, oak. We ran right round the back of the house.

"I'll get my luggage later," said Mr. William. "Can't wait to see Bunty."

I said quickly, "I'll wait here for you. It's very pleasant."

He was round at my door in a flash. "Oh, no, you won't, Miss Smith. No shilly-shallying. I get so tired of it. Don't delay me. In you come."

I felt horribly embarrassed and annoyed and ... well, all mixed up. I just hoped that his lavender-and-mignonette girl told him later what she thought, bringing his secretary with him.

Of course he was sometimes like this in the shop ... exuberant. He had my hand in a grip I could not release. It was making my cameo ring bite into my finger. The back door was open, arched over by a tangle of jessamine twigs that made a fall of sunshine over it where the afternoon sun streamed through the golden petals.

Into a big, old-fashioned kitchen we went, where somebody comfortably broad in the beam was bending over a soup-pot. She straightened up.

Mr. William said, "Oh, Hayley, this is my secretary, the one I told you about ... the Serene Miss Smith. Miss Smith, this is Mrs. Hayle, my gardener's wife, who helps out in the house."

Mrs. Hayle said tartly but with a hint of indulgence in her tone, "And serene she'd need to be, too, to cope with you all day. How do you do, Miss Smith."

Mr. William sniffed. "Jove, that smells good, Hayley." He stirred it with the big wooden spoon, scooped up some, blew on it, tasted it. "It is too." He dipped the spoon back, brought up some more, held it out to me. "Taste it, Miss Smith, but blow on it first."

Mrs. Hayle turned to a drawer. "Mr. William! Talk about hygiene! You'll scandalise Miss Smith!"

He chuckled. "Hayley, that soup's so hot, it'll sterilise any germs I may have."

I took the spoon, laughing helplessly, blew on it and sipped. It was gorgeous.

He dropped the spoon back, clutched my hand again,

said, "Come on . . . Bunty's in her own room, I suppose, Hayley? Good, come on, Miss Smith."

Mrs. Hayle looked at him in a good-humoured sort of way. "Like a whirlwind, he is, always dashing madly through the house." I suppose she had known him since he was a little boy. We took the stairs two at a time under Mr. William's orders. Anything less like my suave draper employer couldn't have been imagined.

As we reached the landing I hissed at him, furious with him for involving me in so unorthodox a position, "I am *not* coming into her bedroom with you!"

"You are, you know," he said, and swept me in to a large, lovely bedroom that looked out to sea. There was a three-quarter bed in it, heaped with pillows, and lying against them a small, rather wizened little woman with sandy hair gone grey and a nutcracker chin!

Mr. William let go my hand, reached the bed, swooped down and planted a kiss on one wrinkled cheek, grabbed her hand and said: "Bunty! You old warhorse! Thrown at last. Now you know what it feels like!"

I knew I was gaping like a fish.

He threw himself down in the easy chair by the bed and gave way to laughter. "Look at her, Bunty! I've scuppered her for once. This is that stiff and starchy secretary of mine that I've told you about. She scares the life out of me. But I've turned the tables this time and no mistake. She thought you were my sweetheart. But then so you are!"

I gulped, swallowed, tried to think what to say. Manse life is a great training-ground for meeting most situations . . . honestly, till you've lived in one you'd never know the fantastic things that can happen any day . . . and do happen. It's not the stodgy existence some folk think it is—but this time I was really at a loss.

Finally I managed: "I—I suppose you're Miss Pamela Huntingdon. I . . . how are you?"

A pair of faded blue eyes surveyed me shrewdly. "Then I expect it was you who ordered those flowers. I wondered when I saw the name . . . nobody's called me Pamela for the last thirty years or so." She turned to

Mr. William. "You deserve to want, Bill. That was a most uncalled-for extravagance...sending a box of flowers right from town by taxi. There's no sense in it."

He grinned unrepentantly. "It wasn't meant to be sensible, you man-eater. It was meant to be a lavish and loving gesture, and you don't deceive me. You loved it!"

He turned to the bedside table and took a sniff at the exquisite basket spilling over with fragrance.

"It was well enough," said Bunty, "but as to this business of ordering a *nurse*. You must be off your head. It's just stuff and nonsense! I'll be up and about in a couple of days."

"Oh no, you won't. I rang Robertshaw from Auckland and got the lowdown on your injury."

"You've got more money than sense." Bunty was unyielding.

Mr. William said: "Where is the nurse, anyway? You know you ought not to talk like that, Bunty my love, you might hurt her feelings."

"Hurt her feelings!" said Bunty witheringly. "You couldn't hurt her feelings with a bludgeon. She'd only humour me and say soothingly: 'I know, I know... being laid aside when we are active is apt to make us a little crotchety.'"

Mr. William chuckled. "I'm sorry for that nurse trying to tend you—where did you say she was?"

"I didn't. But she's off for a walk through the bush. I thought she needed fresh air. And I needed a spell from her tongue. Not that she's all that bad at bandaging and whatnot, as far as nurses go, but—"

"But me no buts. Bunty, I've never enjoyed anything as much as my recent verbal clash with my secretary. My prim and proper Miss Smith thought you were my latest fancy! She even asked me what shade your hair was. I told her it was the latest shade...silver-gilt."

Goaded, I said: "Silver-gilt's been advertised for years, as you ought to know—you run a beauty salon."

Mr. William gave me as dark a look as a man so cheerful could achieve. "That's the one department I stay

away from. They can have it. Come and take my chair,
Miss Smith, and get acquainted with our Bunty. I'll
dash down and bring us up a tray of afternoon tea."

Slightly bemused, I took the chair. I felt decidedly
scared of this Bunty. She burst into a cackle of laughter.

"That boy! But he's got to work off his spirits somehow, cooped up all day in the rag trade."

She had the same indulgent tone I'd noticed in Mrs.
Hayle. I forbore to point out that he'd hardly been
cooped up today, flying in perfect weather on that
dream-trip from Auckland to Dunedin with both
islands spread below him like a relief map.

It was a delicious afternoon tea. An old-fashioned
one—home-made bread off a cottage loaf with a floury,
crisp crust, cut thin and buttered; spicy Chelsea buns,
also home-made, in white and brown wheels. Not fancy
china, either, but big plain gold and white cups with
a clover-leaf in the centre of the saucer. Something
about it appealed to me, perhaps because it was so
different from the shop where everything was as up-
to-date as tomorrow.

The feeling of strain began to wear off. It was just
like country parish visiting. I couldn't help liking Bunty.
You felt you knew where you were with these no-non-
sense people.

There was a heavier footfall downstairs and a shout:
"Bill, are you there? Bi-ill? Oh, good. Look, come and
give me a hand, will you? The Old Warrior's stuck.
It'll need two pairs of hands and your hefty shoulders."

Mr. William gulped down the last of his tea, excused
himself, and disappeared.

The nurse came back and made short work of me,
insisting that Bunty looked tired, so I found myself
banished downstairs to Mrs. Hayle's kitchen.

As I reached the door Bunty said, scowling, "Come
you back next week, Miss Smith, when this tyrant will
be gone. I was just enjoying my bit crack with you."

I heard the nurse chuckle.

I hoped nervously that Mr. William would not be
long. I could be in the way here. But Mrs. Hayle made
me most welcome.

"We'll be lucky if Mr. William is back within the hour," she said. "When he and my Ben get going on that green feed cutter that's the joy of their lives, they forget the time."

"Oh, dear," I said, then, "I don't want to hold you up, Mrs. Hayle. Perhaps I could help you."

She made no protestations, simply took an apron from the back of the door and said, "Perhaps you'd like to peel these apples for me. One thing about that nurse, she does appreciate her food. Can't stand finicky folk. I want to make this apple pie and get it out of the oven just ready for reheating before I have to put the steak in."

I was slicing the last apple into the saucepan when Mr. William came back in, earlier than expected. He'd changed before going out into the poultry run and wore indescribable boots and khaki overalls.

"I won't be long, Miss Smith." He wasn't.

I'd decided we'd be lucky if we got an hour back at the shop, but what I hadn't bargained on was a puncture.

Mr. William grimaced. "Haven't had a puncture in two years and it has to happen now! Oh, well, I guess there's never a convenient time for a puncture."

I helped him. Then before Waitati we struck a huge mob of sheep. As we reached the motorway he glanced at his watch. "We'll reach town dead on five-thirty. No sense in going back to the shop. I'll run you straight home."

I said quickly: "You can drop me in the Octagon. We live right up the hill."

"I know. It's St. Adrian's Manse at West Hill, isn't it?"

"Yes, but there's no point in making yourself any later. If I know anything about nurses they're demons for punctuality and time-tables, and you'll upset Mrs. Hayle's stuffed steak and apple pie."

"Miss Smith, don't be so obstructive. You take a delight in thwarting me. It's a contrary streak in your nature I don't care for!" He was laughing. "It will take me exactly twenty minutes extra all told. It's a poor household that can't postpone dinner twenty minutes."

I gave up.

It would have been fine if Father hadn't been coming back from parish visiting just as we drew up, and manse life gets you into such a habit of hospitality that you can't help overdoing it. After all, this was my *boss*. There was no need at all for Dad to say, beaming, "Come on in and meet my wife." *Or* for Mr. William to accept. I know he did it only to annoy me. As we walked up the path with Father ahead, Mr. William had the nerve to put his hand under my elbow and say in a low voice, "Fair enough ... you meet my household, I meet yours." I wouldn't answer.

There was only one thing I hoped ... that Mother would remember he was my boss and make it brief. I also hoped she was flat out in the kitchen and had an early meeting in the offing so it would be just a case of hullo and goodbye, nice to have met you.

It wasn't.

Mother was sitting in the living-room with the table beautifully set, looking relaxed and charming, seated in an easy chair opposite someone I knew only too well. He rose and said, "Oh, Serena, how nice to see you."

Lance Reedway! When had he flown down? And why? Three days ago Mr. William had been sitting next him at the Master Drapers' dinner in the North Island. And why, oh, why was he here, of all places? He'd never met my people all the time I'd been at Reedway's. What a day!

Mother beamed. Situations are never awkward for Mother. She is always so sublimely convinced that all is well, that somehow you find yourself accepting everything as being for the very best in this best of all possible worlds.

"Lance has come down for the varsity year here, dear, and didn't realise Knox College wasn't open yet, not till tomorrow. He doesn't know a soul but us, so he rang me up to find out if I could recommend a hotel for him to stay at, so—"

I finished it for her, rather limply, "So of course

he's going to stay the night at the Manse." It was inevitable. Mother couldn't help herself. But as for getting on to Christian name terms as soon as this . . . well, really ! And that grinning, handsome bounder, Lance Reedway, would take full advantage of her natural hospitality.

I managed to greet him fairly equably with only a hint of reproach in my eye, with my face out of Mother's range of vision.

Mr. William, of course, greeted him most urbanely. Then he said to Mother in the most ordinary tone as if it was nothing out of the way, and as if he always called me by my Christian name, "I had Serena out at Tattoo Bluff this afternoon. We meant to get back to the office in time to put an hour's work in, but my man had a bit of trouble with a machine, so it made us late; then we had a puncture, to say nothing of meeting a huge mob of sheep, so I brought Serena straight home."

"Yes, of course," said Mother, not even bothering to ask why it had been necessary to have his secretary out at his estate. "What a lovely change for Serena. I'm sure she must have enjoyed it. You'll stay for dinner, of course, Mr. Durbridge?"

I started to say no, he couldn't, but wasn't quick enough. He said, "Thanks very much, I'd like to, if it won't put you out? Oh, good, then may I just use your phone to let them know I'll not be home till much later?"

Much.

I swallowed, said instantly, "Mr. William, won't Bunty be looking for a yarn with you?"

He grinned. "She's having the time of her life arguing with that nurse."

I gave up.

The sense of unreality pursued me right through the meal, but before that I followed Mother into the kitchen and said : "Have we got enough?"

"Yes. Patsy rang to say she's staying in town tonight and going out with one of the teachers. And it just happened I'd done a very large casserole of chops, thinking I could just reheat what was left tomorrow night. I've thrown in some extra frozen peas and tomatoes and I'd made a double-sized apple pasty so I could have some for cutting into squares for the A.P.W. meeting tomorrow afternoon. But I'd like you to slip down to the dairy for a bottle of cream."

I said, rather shortly, "He can have just milk on his pudding . . . crashing in on us like this."

Mother gazed at me in surprise. "Serena! Now, here's the bottle, dear, and just get right down for that cream. And get a big pack of ice-cream."

I took the bottle, then halted dead in my tracks as Mother added: "Imagine Lance Reedway thinking of going into the ministry! Isn't it nice?"

I turned slowly, said, "What? I don't believe it. You've got it wrong."

"No, I haven't. He's got two more years varsity to get through before he can get into the Theological Hall, of course. It seems that after you left Reedway's and took that temporary job in Auckland, he did a year up there. I'm so pleased. When a man that age decides to go in for the ministry it's usually serious, not a sudden decision. And it's good for any minister to have ordinary working years behind him."

I felt more mixed up than ever.

At the door I bumped into Debbie, racing in with Spot, our super mongrel.

I collared the dog and shoved him in the laundry. Then I handed Debbie the bottle and the money, told her to go to the dairy and said: "And when you come back for goodness' sake get that paint off your face. We've got my boss for dinner, heaven help me . . . *and* my Auckland boss."

Debbie stared. "Gosh, is it a bang-up affair, then? You don't look pleased, Serena. Don't you like them?"

I looked at her sourly. "Liking doesn't come into it. You just endure bosses . . . or so I've found. Now scram, and don't forget that wash."

Debbie tossed her pony-tail over her shoulder. "It won't be a bit of use. Our teacher's been instructing us in the art of Maori carving and we've used the proper paints—staining really. It lasts for ever. Quite indelible."

And she was gone.

Mother had gone back into the living-room and was offering drinks of apple juice and soda water. I could have had hysterics. I was sure Mr. William had never had that before dinner in his life. Served him right!

I said: "Delay dinner just a few moments, would you, Mother? That child has got what she says is indelible paint all over her face. They've been doing Maori carvings. I'll probably have to remove half her skin."

Mr. William said, "Oh, leave her be, Serena. Why don't you relax? You aren't at the office now." I could have choked him.

CHAPTER THREE

THE paint did stay on—mostly—but I got all the dirt off. I made Debbie change out of her indescribable trews into a blue frock and an Alice band. With her shining pale gold hair and deep blue eyes my little sister looked too good to be true.

Mother was foolish enough to put her next Mr. William. He and Debbie immediately embarked on a discussion of Maori carvings and the artifacts at Tattoo Point.

When they paused for a moment, Debbie said: "Listen to poor Spot howling his head off. Serena shut him in the laundry."

Mr. William said: "Is he used to occupying the hearthrug?"

Debbie nodded. "Yes, always. I don't know what's got into Serena. It mixes a dog up, doesn't it? Gets him confused in his relationship patterns with the family . . . inside one moment, banished the next!"

Mr. William said consoling, "I expect Serena is a little shattered because she's entertaining her boss, feeling that things should be just so . . . but I'm a farmer really. How about it, Serena, don't you think that we could be kind to that poor dumb animal and let him in?"

I looked things unlawful to be uttered, and Dad, laughing, said, "Go get him, Debbie, but don't touch him or you'll have to scrub up all over again."

I said in a low voice as Debbie passed my chair, "But don't feed him in here."

Dad heard it and said, "You're fighting a losing battle, dear child."

I kept on automatically helping Mother and keeping Lance and Mr. William supplied with condiments, cream, sugar, but moved as if in a dream. Lance Reedway going in for the ministry, and my boss sitting opposite me at the manse table, positively encouraging Debbie and that dog!

So much for trying to keep my business life and private life apart. I could have shaken my parents. They were so sublimely unaware that it mattered to me, and Lance and Mr. William were falling for Mother in a big way. She was encouraging them to talk about themselves and was so natural. I suddenly wanted to giggle, and with that relief from tension I was swept with a wave of love for her. Mother could cope with anything.

Dad said he'd once seen her involved in a quite horrible family quarrel in a parish, without turning a hair. "And oddly enough, Serena, the people concerned were never—afterwards—embarrassed with her. It usually works out that way, you know. Even if you are able to extricate folk out of their difficulties, they often resent you knowing so much about them. But not your mother. She was just as unconcerned as she would be— I predict—if she were invited to Buckingham Palace. All part of her calm acceptance of everything as part of an interesting world."

No wonder everyone told my mother their troubles. She'd probably have Lance Reedway's sorted out in no time. But heaven send she kept away from Mr. William's. I really did not want him part of this family circle. I preferred him a little remote. Why? My mind flinched from that question. Why indeed? Perhaps I knew, even then, that he had the power to disturb me that no one else had.

I did hope, though, that he'd get away before Patsy came home. Bad enough for her morale to know that one man had followed me right from Auckland to Dunedin without finding my present boss one of the group also.

Oddly enough, when I managed to forget the components of the party, we got on very nicely, with Lance and Mr. William having enough common interests to keep the conversational ball rolling.

The lovely long Dunedin twilight lingered long enough for us to sit on in the lounge without lights and to leave the windows open to the heavenly scents of the garden. Mother had night-scented stock and lavender under all the windows.

Presently Mother, Father, and Mr. William became absorbed in some topic, and Lance, sitting near me on the window-seat, said in a low voice, "Serena, your mother warned me to say nothing when you came in . . . but what in the world possessed you to dye your beautiful hair?"

I said quickly, "Same reason as most women . . . I wanted a change," and leaned forward and said to Father, "Are you right on that, Dad? I thought it happened when we lived in New Plymouth."

Dad shook his head. "Wasn't it when we lived up in Bay of Islands? At least—Oh, I know how we can settle that. Serena, hop off that window-seat, will you?"

He lifted the squab, then the lid, and dived in, turning photos over rapidly, then said : "It'll be in this lot."

He knelt on the carpet right in front of Mr. William and scattered the photographs looking for what he wanted. Well, it had served to head Lance off the subject of my hair.

Mr. William leaned forward, picked up a large coloured photograph of Douglas's wedding, at which I'd been a bridesmaid, and said : "Good heavens, your hair is sheer gold in this, Serena. Did you dye it that colour for the wedding?"

I was struck dumb.

Father wasn't. "No, girls are downright daft these days. I pride myself on understanding the youth of today, but why a girl with glorious hair like Serena's wants to tint it a dull fawn is quite beyond me. And I've said so. Her hair is naturally like Deborah's."

Over his head my eyes met Mr. William's.

He nodded. "So you *are* a blonde!"

I knew I was scarlet. That I'd have to give one of the reasons why. I was bowled out properly. But I wouldn't bring Patsy into it. Not even Mother and Father had guessed how deeply that had gone. I didn't want to cause them any anguish. They would hate to think there was a rift in the family lute. So I summoned up a grin, twinkled at Lance and said, "Well, since your mother was so devastatingly frank with my present employer, I can say why? Women just naturally suspect blonde secretaries, and I've been more unfortunate than most.

"You didn't know, Lance, when I applied to you, but while Mr. Franton, my first boss, gave me time to get another job, so he didn't have to put that giveaway phrase on my reference : 'Miss Smith leaves us owing to the reorganisation of our staff arrangements,' I really was sacked. I lost my job because Mrs. Fanton didn't trust blondes ! By the time I had the flare-up with *your* mother, Lance, I really had had it.

"And I've enjoyed being mouse. I've found the staff much more friendly than any I've worked with. Blondes are always suspect. So that's fine and the discussion ends. I stay mouse."

I tried to look casually at Mr. William, but as soon as I did I had to look away. I didn't know why.

I was deeply thankful that at that moment the door opened and Patsy came in.

For myself I've always liked dark brown hair much better than gold. Patsy's is like a shining cap, and when the sun or the lamplight glints on it it's like sunlight shining on the flanks of a chestnut mare, something that never fails to delight me. I think that gentle-men who prefer blondes must be quite, quite mad.

But tonight I really stared at Patsy. She seemed different, she looked simply beautiful—no other word for it. She's usually pale, but she had a flake of carna-tion pink in each cheek and her soft pansy-brown eyes were lit up ... in fact she had a completely incandes-cent look about all of her. What—

"Oh, hullo, Patsy," said Mother. "I thought you might not be in for ages. I thought perhaps you and this teacher might have gone to the pictures."

"No, this teacher had a lot of marking to do. We simply had tea and then took a run round the harbour as far as Portobello and watched the moon rise over Harbour Cone."

"How nice ... dear, this is Lance Reedway ... yes, Serena's former boss, who has come down to Knox College; and this is Mr. Durbridge, Serena's new chief."

Patsy dimpled and flashed a look at me. "Goodness, aren't you having fun, Serena. I'd find that an ordeal myself. Mother, I hope you never decide to line up all my headmasters for a meal. I just couldn't stand it!"

Both men grinned and Mr. William said, "I don't really regard myself as very new. Not officially speaking anyway. But I think I can regard myself as a new *friend* of Serena's—eh, Serena? She's been keeping me at arms' length ever since she came to me. But I can see the reason for it now. No wonder you tried to keep to a strictly business footing with *me*. But *my* mother is twelve thousand miles away and I haven't got a wife. You're quite safe, Serena, and in no danger of losing your job with Durbridge's."

I was tempted to remind him that it might be differ-ent when his grandmamma came home, but resisted it. I wanted the conversation to get back to the general, instead of keeping to the particular. It did.

I went out and made supper. They could hardly go on discussing my chequered career in my absence.

"I made this rather earlier than usual," I said to Mr. William, "because I feel it's mean keeping you from Bunty all this time." And when he was leaving I said hastily, "You'll see Mr. William to the door, won't you, Father?"

I helped Mother make up Lance Reedway's bed, resenting all the time being forced into such intimate friendliness with him. It put me in an awkward position. Surely Lance wasn't serious about me? Oh, I didn't think I was the cause of his deciding to go into the ministry, I thought *that* had probably sprung out of his associations at varsity in Auckland. No one would make a decision like that on such flimsy grounds, with no encouragement, but I dared not be too friendly. With Mother's passion for mothering all lonely males boarding away from home, I was gloomily sure we were going to see a lot of Mr. Lance Reedway as it was.

Also, I wasn't quite sure how I was going to handle Mr. William Durbridge after this. Men were pests. They so complicated things! It would be so hard to go on being his Serene Miss Smith. He knew now it was only a protective veneer.

I found Patsy and Lance deep in discussion so tiptoed out again, a wild hope stirring. Wouldn't it be wonderful if Lance decided he liked her better? What a boost to Patsy's morale that would be!

Father came back from seeing Mr. William off and began to get the milk-bottle to take down to the gate.

"Well, how fortunate you are in your boss, Serena. What a thoroughly likeable fellow."

I gritted my teeth and thought: I just wish you'd seen him out with that brassy Veronica, as I did! I said, in an off-hand tone, "Oh, he's all right, I suppose, but one never feels really enthusiastic about one's boss."

I picked up a tea-towel and began to dry the dishes Mother was washing. Suddenly she paused, hands deep in the soapsuds, "Serena, *is* it usual to go to watch the moon rise with . . . a *girl*-friend?"

I turned and hung a cup up. So Mother had noticed the incandescence too!

"You mean—?" I said slowly.

"I just realised tonight how often lately Patsy has said : 'This teacher.' It's been several times to see a film. Twice to a play and to several lectures. She's never mentioned the teacher by name. So it's not a woman. Serena, why hasn't she brought him home? You—you don't think—oh, no, Patsy wouldn't! She's so open. Yet it's not good that any minister and his wife should think *their* daughter would be above clandestine things. Serena, do you think she's fallen in love with a married man?"

"Patsy? But no. A thousand times no. And if she had, she'd not go out with him. She'd resist it. You know Patsy and her devastating candour. Oh, Mother, Patsy's always been the tell-the-truth-and-shame-the-devil kind. She'd never go in for anything underhand. I think it's just that she's a bit wary, after Mark."

Mother had only known that Mark had lost interest in Patsy, not that he had fancied . . . and pestered . . . me.

Mother wrung the dishcloth out. "I think you might be right, Serena. Darling, do see if she'll talk to you. I don't want to force her confidence. I think the young need their privacy too. Thank goodness Douglas's love-life went so smoothly."

I kissed her goodnight, went in and said goodnight to Patsy, Dad, and Lance, who were still deep in talk, and went to bed, feeling inexpressibly weary.

I'd try to get back on the formal footing with Mr. William. No good ever came of being too matey with one's boss.

I was still reading when Patsy put her heard round the door. "Good, you aren't asleep yet . . . that former boss of yours is much different from what you used to tell about him. I thought him a gay Lothario. You must have been way off beam, pet. A candidate for the ministry, no less."

Something sprang into my mind . . . that old tag : "He was warned against the woman, she was warned against the man, and if that can't make a wedding, then there's nothing else that can."

So I said : "Watch it, Patsy . . . he's a flirt. He may

finish his studies at varsity, but I very much doubt he'll
ever enter the ranks of the ministry. Don't lose your
heart to him."

Patsy stared. Then she laughed. "Serena, your
imagination must have got away with you. Who cares
whether Lance Reedway is a flirt or not? That's not
what I popped in for. Serena, you'd better get that
dye washed out—it's served its purpose."

I looked at her without showing any apprehension
and said : "You mean because of what Mr. William
said, having no mother or wife to worry about? I dared
not remind· him, because he is, after all, my employer,
that he has a very formidable grandmother from all
I hear about her. She's been in the States on this
prolonged business tour and buying spree and hasn't
seen me yet. It was only an odd combination of circumstances that he was here tonight. So I'll stay
mouse."

Patsy flopped on the bed. "Very clever, Serena, very
clever. You don't deceive me one bit. That business
about Mark shook you, didn't it? One look at you and
he forgot me. Serena, you've been the best sort of big
sister a girl could have . . . bar none. I admit I was hurt,
therefore a little bitter, but I got over it so quickly I
realised I couldn't really have loved Mark. I thought
I'd probably stay on in Auckland teaching, but once
I realised it had been all gossamer and moonshine, I
came home as fast as I could.

"It's not your fault that you're so beautiful, Serena,
or that men fall for you. And it's not a bit of good my
thinking it's *bound* to happen again. Only . . . I'd like
to try to—to cement *this* attachment for longer this
time. Mark met you too soon. Yes, I'm in love again.
He teaches out at North Head. I want to be sure of
myself—and him—before I bring this one home.

"But when I do, I want you to be blonde again. To
put him to the test." She flicked my hair and giggled
as she used to do. "If I don't, I'll never have any confidence in myself again. I want him to love me in spite
of my sister's looks."

I said slowly, "Well, when you're ready to bring him

home give me plenty of warning, will you? I want to stay mouse for a while."

Mercifully, Patsy was too taken up with her own affairs to probe.

I added : "There's just one thing, Patsy. You know how astute Mother is? Well, she's tumbled to the fact that 'this teacher' must be a man and she's worried about it. She thought he might have been a married man and that was why you were not bringing him home. You know what Mother is, always afraid of being sure that the children of the manse won't get into trouble just like other sons and daughters?"

Patsy gazed at me. "Oh, help, Serena! What are we going to tell her to put her mind at rest?"

I had an inspiration. "I know. I'll tell her that you felt the whole family, including yourself, took the affair of Mark too seriously, too soon. That you feel if you bring this one home too early, he'll feel he's being looked over. That you're not sure of your own feelings—that you realise you fell in love again very soon and you want to sort yourself out before this one is brought into the bosom of the family."

Patsy gazed at me with great respect and flung her arms about me. "Serena, that's positively brilliant!" I felt a great load slip off my heart. This was how we used to be before this horrible situation had cropped up.

Suddenly she held me off and surveyed my face searchingly.

"Serena, something's happened to you? Have you fallen in love?"

I could feel the colour beginning to rise and knew that in a moment she would say : "You're in love with your boss!" So what she did say set me gaping.

"Aren't you the cunning one? You always said that Lance Reedway was spoiled by being under his mother's thumb and that he'd not amount to a tin of fish if he stayed in a job he knew he couldn't lose. You didn't fancy being married to a draper whose mother held the reins, did you? And you were courageous enough to take the risk of breaking off with him altogether.

Good for you! And it's paid dividends. He's broken away from Mamma and taken up one of the toughest callings he could ... the ministry! Serena, you'd make a wonderful minister's wife."

I gazed at her blankly. "*Me*? Patsy, you must be mad. Why, I'd be the last person in the world for that position. Besides, I know far too much about manse life, thanks."

"Don't be ridiculous. Look at Mother. She's not an orthodox minister's wife at all, but she loves every minute of it."

"Patsy, don't you realise that to Mother, life *is* Father? His life is hers. I'm too much of an individualist. I couldn't suffer fools gladly like Mother does; I couldn't be tolerant with the intolerant, or love the unlovely, either. Mother has depths in her nature that I haven't."

My little sister looked at me in a way I'd never seen her look before, and what she said made me realise that those few brief months away from us last year had matured her. That the two years between us had suddenly disappeared.

"Serena, you don't imagine Mother was always like this, do you? Isn't it that the years have mellowed her? Experience. I think you and Lance Reedway would make a wonderful pair. Your business background would be a common meeting-ground. Dad and he would have kindred interests if he's set on the Church, and honestly, he'd be a dazzler in gown and bands. If your ideal of a minister's wife is Mother as she is now, you've never seen her as a person at all, only as a parent."

I put my arms round Patsy, laughed into her pansy-brown eyes, said, "Patsy, in some ways you're now older than I am. It's fascinating. Being in love—truly in love—has done something for you, hasn't it? But you're way off beam about me and Lance Reedway. I've never felt for him anything more than a sort of loyal attachment such as I felt for most of the staff at Reedway's."

Patsy got off the bed, stood looking down on me.

"Serena, haven't you ever been in love? I mean it seems so odd—at your'age."

I looked down, smoothed out the bedclothes. I said, "I can't be made of the stuff of romance, Patsy. No, I've never been in love."

And as she went out of the room, I said to myself. "Not till now . . . and much good it will do you, Serena Smith!"

CHAPTER FOUR

MOTHER was completely convinced and relieved when I told her Patsy's reluctance to bring home this mysterious teacher was simply that she wanted to be sure of herself.

Mother looked sage. "I can understand it. Families can be embarrassing, look knowing, tease . . . and it can rub a little of the dream-dust off. It's a good thing for young folk to see each other's backgrounds, but not too soon. Nobody likes things to be taken for granted. You remember Mrs. Hartington and how she scared off all Eunice's boy-friends by inquiring into their prospects as soon as Eunice brought one home? It was as good as asking their intentions. And in the end Eunice got so sick of it, she went off to Australia on a working holiday and married there. Well, Serena, it's put my mind at rest. I'll tell your Father. He's been a bit worried too."

Then I said what I'd made up my mind to say, "And, Mother, with regard to *my* affairs. I don't want Lance Reedway encouraged to come here too often. In fact I'd prefer it if he didn't come at all."

Mother looked at me out of the clear blue eyes that only Debbie had inherited and said, "Serena, *I* certainly won't, but I'm afraid your father has already asked him to take over the Boys' Club for games. You know they need a new leader. And he said to me that if he thinks—on longer acquaintance—that he's the man

for the job, he'll ask him to take on the Intermediate
Bible Class Leadership when Barrie Thornton gets
transferred to Wellington."

I felt utterly dismayed. Then I said, as philosophic-
ally as I could manage, "Well, I'll just have to be sure
I give him no personal encouragement whatever. I
mean it wouldn't be fair to him. I feel so darned responsible, Mother. I don't mean I'm vain enough to
think he'd do all this because of me, and I believe he's
tremendously sincere, but it seems to be those horribly
snobbish words of mine, uttered in temper, that got him
on the raw and started all this off. Oh, Mother, talk
about life and death in the power of the tongue!"

Mother said, "Now, Serena, don't get yourself into
a state. We all say things in angry moments that we'd
give anything to recall, and surely, if this suddenly
triggered Lance Reedway into taking stock of himself,
deciding to take life in a more responsible fashion—he
told me he was just frittering his time away at the
shop—then you'll have done good, not harm.

"Mind you, that doesn't mean you need feel any
responsibility towards him. And you'll have to be careful not to encourage him. In fact—" a gleam shot into
Mother's eye. Her whole face lit up. I knew the signs
and my heart sank. Mother had had an Idea.

"Yes, it would be a good idea to let him think your
affections were already engaged! Then he couldn't
harbour any false hopes. I mean that lovely boss of
yours, Mr. William. Now, that's the idea, Serena. I'll
drop Lance a hint, very, very subtly, of course, that you
and Mr. William are interested in each other. Come
to think of it, I suspected that very thing tonight. He
said he'd probably be seeing more of us. And—"

I took my dear, darling, terrible mother by her
elbows and said sternly : "Catherine Melisande Smith!
You will do nothing of the kind. Mr. William Durbridge got here by accident, practically, and I never
want to see him in the Manse again! No, thank you.
Now, Mother, this job at Durbridge's I want to keep.
It's well paid and it's a good firm—happy atmosphere
among the staff and so on. And the surest way to lose

a job—as I've proved—is to tangle with the management. I'm not having any. Life has been complicated enough for me that way. And I wouldn't trust Mr. William as far as I could see him. He's having a quite violent affair with the most artificial blonde you could imagine . . . loads her with presents. One Veronica Boleyn. So hands off, I'll handle Lance myself. Now I must go to bed, this is my second attempt. I just came out to set your mind at rest about Patsy and all I've done is get you mixed up about me! Goodnight, Pet, and God bless."

Though I really felt like saying: "God help us all if Mother tries her hand at stratagems and spoils!"

As I got to the door Mother's soft voice called me back.

"Serena?"

"Yes?"

"*I would*, you know."

I was mystified. "You would *what*?"

"Trust Mr. William as far as I could see him . . . and further. And I like him much the better of the two. Goodnight, Serena, sleep well."

But Mother, like Macbeth, had murdered sleep.

For I knew only too well that Mother, despite her enjoyment of life with Father, had always said she wanted none of her girls to marry ministers. We'd tackled her about it once, laughingly.

She'd gone all serious on it. Had said, quite wistfully, "I know. There's no other life for me. But almost all parents hope—perhaps foolishly—that life will be a little easier for their children than it was for them, and . . . well, I'm every bit as foolish as any parent."

I felt a deep unease at the memory. I had an idea that Mother was seeing in Lance a threat to the kind of future she hoped I might have. She wanted me to live a life of my own, a private life.

She might think I could, eventually, be touched by the thought that Lance had given up a much more moneyed and certainly easier existence, for my sake. And she had fallen heavily for Mr. William's undoubted charm.

Even as I had.

The knowledge I'd refused to face all this time rose up and hit me.

There was no future in it. Because he wasn't good husband material. I didn't think he'd ever be serious about any woman. He'd just regard me as he regarded Veronica Boleyn . . . as a decorative companion.

I admired many things about him, his courtesy with his staff (but no doubt he found that paid off) and his obvious fondness for Bunty (but then she was necessary to his welfare) and his unfailing good humour. But what did those things add up to? Not necessarily strength of character.

I thumped the pillow and turned it over once more. These men that went for looks! Odd how plain girls always envied pretty ones. Maybe they didn't have such a good time at parties and dances, but at least when someone fell in love with them they could be sure they were loved for themselves, for their personalities, and that it would last. That was something none of them ever thought about, I imagined.

Oh, well, I was going to have to keep both Mr. William and Lance at a distance. I turned over again and offered up the queerest little prayer. But then I'm sure God is used to queer prayers, and unravels them. I just said : "Please, God, send along somebody ordinary. Somebody who'll love *me*, not my looks." And I fell forty fathoms deep into the most refreshing sleep.

Isn't it a good thing God sees deeper than our spoken prayers? That He finds out our real needs and answers those? But this profound thought only occurred to me much later, not just then. I had a long way to go.

Of course in the morning things were blessedly ordinary. Drama doesn't flourish in the breakfast hour. And the morning at Durbridge's was most uneventful.

As I settled at my desk Mr. William said : "And how is my Serene Miss Smith, this morning?"

I said, shortly, "Serene, as usual. Mr. William, those indent forms for the baby-linen department are here.

Miss Lucas asked me as I came in if I would get you to check them."

What a wonderfully reassuring effect routine had on you. Yesterday and all its surprises was far away. I didn't even ask how Bunty was, though I felt mean omitting it. I just didn't want to bring the too-personal back into our relationship, for I knew Mr. William would take full advantage of it.

It was very busy till eleven, with travellers in and out, buyers trying to get a few moments alone with their chief, the accountant pinning him down to figures and a lot of dictation to be taken.

Then the pressure eased. Mr. William looked across from his desk. "Serena, let me give you lunch." He grinned. "I promise you we won't argue over this one."

"We certainly won't, Mr. William. I'm not having lunch with you, but thank you all the same."

"Your politeness is almost devastating and freezes me to the marrow. Why won't you have lunch with me?"

I regarded him over the top of my typewriter as one might a persistent child. Actually I felt quite proud of myself, standing up to my boss in this manner. Or so I told myself. Deep down I think I knew that as an employer Mr. William would not hold it against me, that he was pressing this as a man.

"Why won't I lunch with you, Mr. William? Same reason as before . . . I just don't care to."

"Your candour is as chilling as your politeness . . . except, of course, that I just don't believe you."

I rolled a quite unnecessary sheet of paper into my machine.

"Your vanity, Mr. William, is beyond belief."

I could have choked him when he laughed. There was genuine amusement in it.

Goaded, I said : "Well, if that isn't my reason, what do you suppose I turned you down for?"

The sherry-brown eyes met mine, with sheer devilment in them.

"Because, my dear Miss Smith, you're a little afraid of yourself."

"Afraid of myself?" I was annoyed to hear my voice squeak a little with surprise and indignation.

"Yes. You're not quite sure if you can handle me."

I was so cross I couldn't speak. I swallowed and counted ten. Then I said as coldly as I could at the moment, "Mr. William, I've an appointment to get my hair done at ten past twelve. I'll be having a sandwich and a cup of tea under the dryer."

His eyes were mocking. "A much more credible reason. Better for my ego, too."

"There's nothing wrong with your ego, Mr. William. It seems to me to be in a very healthy state."

He tilted his chair back and roared with laughter.

"Your verbal ability, Miss Smith, fills me with admiration and delight. Some blondes are beautiful but dumb. You are anything but dumb. Well, if you have an engagement at lunch-time, how about—"

"And I have an engagement tonight too, thank you."

He looked at me reproachfully. "I wasn't asking if I could take you out tonight. I couldn't. I have a date."

I couldn't resist it. "Veronica's turn, is it?"

"I have a date with someone much more bewitching than Veronica, whose charms are only too synthetic and obvious." Our eyes caught and held and I triumphed over the desire to laugh with him. I said patiently, "You're wanting me to go green-eyed over that. From the look in your eye I expect it's someone like Bunty! I'm not to be caught twice."

"It's someone not in the least like Bunty, Miss Omniscience."

Before I could retort the phone rang. When Mr. William found out who it was, his voice softened to a most incredibly tender note. "Molly, how good to hear you. No, I don't want to be thanked. It was nothing, my dear. I even found it fun. She fell for it, hook, line and sinker."

Suddenly I found I had a nasty taste in my mouth. I got up, seized some papers and went down to the showroom. They could have waited till this afternoon, but it gave me the chance to let William Durbridge have his beastly private conversation to himself. He was outrageous!

At twelve he said to me: "You're having your hair-dye washed out, are you?"

I was surprised. "No, why should I?"

"Wasn't it a protection against a susceptible employer?"

I sighed. "It was an endeavour—after two unpleasant experiences—to keep my business life and my private life separate. I thought it was the blonde hair doing it."

"No, Serena. There's much more to you than blonde hair. Ever watch that television programme, 'The Farmer's Daughter'? The girl who is governess to the congressman's sons?"

"Yes, I love it. Why?"

"Katie is blonde, isn't she, a Scandinavian blonde. But her charm doesn't depend on her hair, does it? It's her whole bewitching personality. Come to think of it, you're extremely like her."

I dropped my eyes because I'd realised something in a split second . . . Mr. William was extremely like Congressman Morley in that series, only darker, but the eyes—I clamped down on the thought.

I said instead, wearily, "Mr. William, please! I get distressed by all this. I would so like to be more imper-sonal. Could we not go back to our former relation-ship? You're just a tease and a flirt. It never pays for a secretary to be other than a business connection. It worked before. I had more peace of mind when first I worked for you."

I couldn't, to my confusion, quite hold his eyes. I turned abruptly away, picked up my bag, and went.

It was heavenly to be having a quiet night at home. Mother was going out to an exhibition of paintings with a friend; Father cared very little for such things, so was puffing away at his pipe, serenely glad there were no meetings and hoping—probably vainly—that there'd be no callers, no telephone messages, because it was a good night for television. Patsy was out and Debbie was doing her homework.

It was a little cooler tonight, the first indication that this glorious Otago autumn would end in winter. Dunedin summers were chancy affairs, but February and March were glorious months, with long, still, hot days. In Central Otago the autumn colourings were patching the landscape with living gold and burning russet.

I got into some ancient brown velvet trews and a green jersey of the same vintage.

Mother frowned a little as I settled in one of the big chairs. "Serena, why didn't you keep that suit on? It's so much more feminine, dear."

Father looked up from the crossword he was endeavouring to finish before the news came on, "Oh, leave the girl alone, Catherine. She's comfortable in those, and Serena never looks anything but feminine whatever she wears."

Mother said, quite tartly for her, "Well, she certainly doesn't look feminine with her feet propped up against the mantelpiece like that."

I giggled. "I don't know that I'm so set on being feminine, anyway, Mother. What on earth's got into you tonight? Better be off, pet, I heard a car stop a few seconds back. You're going with Mrs. Abercorne, I suppose, to this—"

Well, it wasn't Mrs. Abercorne. Mother had left the front door open; we heard a brief twang of the doorbell and in strode Mr. William Durbridge. I didn't get time to get my feet down before he was in. But I brought them down mighty smartly after that. I just boggled. Really, he was the limit!

"Mr. William, what on earth are you doing here? What do you want me for?"

He smiled most urbanely. "I don't—want *you*, I mean. I'm taking your mother to that exhibition, Serena. I gather it's not in your line or I'd invite you along with us. Ready, Mrs. Smith?" And he tucked his hand in Mother's elbow.

I daresay Mother felt like smacking me as I said, as awkwardly and obviously as a teenager, "I'll leave some supper out for you, Mother. I'm dead-beat. I'm going early to bed with my library book."

"How nice for you," said Mr. William sweetly. "I must be working you too hard. But don't barge off on my account. This is quite an affair tonight. A reception to visiting artists as well and supper is laid on. Goodnight, Mr. Smith. Goodnight, Serena."

As the door closed behind them Father removed his pipe hurriedly and burst into a great guffaw. "I do like that young man. He knows exactly what he wants and he has no inhibitions whatever. That served you right, Serena!"

I got up, saying, "He certainly hasn't any inhibitions. But I *have*. As for knowing what he wants, it boils down to him wanting very badly what he can't have! And I just wish my matchmaking mother would stay out of this. I'm going to bed. Goodnight, Father."

His chuckles followed me out of the room.

Next morning I did not mention the exhibition. Neither did Mother, though her expression was as bland as cream and her eyes were too innocent for words. Nor did Mr. William mention it.

The next few days were quite uneventful and all devoted to routine work. I told myself I was thankful.

When a fortnight went by I realised that to my immense surprise Mr. William had taken my declaration of wanting to keep business and private life separate really seriously.

It was another matter with Lance Reedway. I got very tired of him being so much at the Manse and took to going out with some of the girls from the staff whenever I knew he was coming. The trouble was I did not always know, but I kept turning down his invitations.

Besides, what really annoyed me was that just when Patsy was becoming more sure of herself, this constant attendance upon me—or my home—would underline the fact that blondes were attractive—even dyed mouse! Because of course Patsy knew Lance thought of me as blonde.

Patsy showed no signs yet of wanting to bring her teacher friend home.

I was feeling terribly restless. Patsy did a lot of preparation for her classes at home and often got me to help, looking up history, or typing poems for her pupils. It woke old yearnings in me. Now Dad was so fit again, after that long spell off preaching, I might be able to take up at varsity again, if I got a part-time job. I had a fair bit saved. I felt it might be better for me if I were right away from drapery and from all complications with bosses.

If I did, then went High School teaching, I'd jolly well make sure I didn't go to a co-ed one. All female staff for me. Yet I thought wistfully that years ago, when I'd no thought that I wouldn't be able to finish my degree, I'd always longed to teach in a co-ed. One of the lovely new ones. I suppose it was because my leaning was towards boys...I'd rather coach cricket than tennis.

I spent quite a wearing fortnight deciding whether or not to make the break from clerical duties immediately, as in New Zealand the varsity year starts in March, but finally I woke up one morning, knowing that I wouldn't leave Durbridge's unless I was sacked. I wouldn't analyse my feelings. I only knew I couldn't. I might have done it had Mr. William continued to pester me, but as things were, back on the old employer-employee footing, I thought I could take it.

I told myself I had been absolutely sensible turning down his every approach. Not for me the butterfly type of man. Some girls would have been flattered, bowled over. No, I was far too sensible. I would just go serenely on.

CHAPTER FIVE

IT was a Friday afternoon. Things were going fine ...
if a little dull. Mr. William hadn't called me anything
but Miss Smith for a long time.

Suddenly the office door flew open and in came a
really elegant figure, brown-eyed, fair-haired, one of
the most attractive women I've ever seen, quite young,
and, clinging to her hand, a miniature of herself.

She stopped short, said: "Bill!" and sprang at
him.

He said: "Kitty!" and sprang at her. I experienced
all sorts of sensations, none of them pleasant, during
the time before Mr. William disentangled himself,
stooped to the poppet, swung her on high and said:
"Can this be my baby niece? Good life, you are a young
lady, Wilhelmina!"

Suddenly his tone altered, sharpened. "Sis, what's
the matter? You're crying! What—"

I stood up, pushed my chair back, and prepared to
beat a retreat. Mr. William's voice halted me, the voice
of authority. "Serena, you're to stay."

I stood stock still. Mr. William's sister lifted her head
from his chest where she had dropped it, and said, "It's
Jeff. I thought you might have heard. He's been injured
in Antarctica. They're flying him back. They couldn't
leave yesterday because of the weather. He'd written
me he'd be back at base soon—end of the good weather,
asked me to come to Christchurch and take a flat. I
flew from San Francisco. I didn't tell you because I
wanted to surprise you and Bunty. But when I got to
Headquarters in Christchurch, I heard that Jeff was
badly injured ... he fell down a crevasse in a Snowcat.

"He'll get here—at least to Christchurch—tonight.
That's the earliest they could make it. It's his skull
and back." She swallowed. "It will be no place for
Wilhelmina. I'll stay at Jeff's side at the hospital. But
she's an adaptable wee soul, and not shy. I thought all
I could do was bring her to Bunty. Only there's no
time to go out to the Bluff. I've got to get the next

plane back. They arranged for a special car to meet me at Momona and take me back. They're waiting out the back of the shop."

I had the strength of it now . . . I'd heard Mr. William had a sister who had married an American scientist who was spending a season at the South Pole.

Mr. William caught his sister against him, patted her shoulder, said, "Sis, how damnable," then, blankly, "and Bunty's got an injured leg. She's laid up."

I saw Kitty's face look absolutely dismayed and could have shot him. He could have kept quiet.

I said, very quickly, "Mr. William, it's the weekend. I'll look after your niece. I'm used to my brother's two wee ones and Mother is marvellous with all children."

A light leapt into Mr. William's eye, and I, contrary fool that I am, was glad to see it. It flooded me with warmth.

Kitty swung round and appraised me as any mother would whose child has to be left with strangers. Then she said slowly : "That's a very nice gesture, I'm sure." She swung back on her brother. Her voice broke a little. "It—it's just that I thought of her as being so—so safe and happy in the old home with Bunty. I—oh, how foolish of me," she turned back to me and I saw that the brown eyes were swimming in tears. "But Bill couldn't manage her alone. He's never had anything to do with tiny ones . . . I think this is one time when I'll just have to depend upon strangers. I've got old school-friends here, but there's no time to contact them."

For the first time she seemed to sag a little. She looked at her watch. "Bill, I just must be there when Jeff's plane gets in. If he's going to come round, even briefly, I must be there."

I heard Mr. William swallow too. We were both aware Kitty wanted to be there, to exchange a goodbye, if that was all she was going to have, with Jeff.

Mr. William managed to say evenly, "Yes, of course, Kitty." He looked at me over her head. "Serena, you'll come out to Tattoo Bluff with Wilhelmina, won't you?

For the weekend or longer. Bunty and Hayley are there as duennas. In fact your mother could come too. Or is she tied up at the church?" He turned to Kitty. "Serena is a minister's daughter."

That seemed to ease Kitty's mind still more.

Mr. William was holding my eyes again. "Of course I will, Mr. William," I said. "Just as long as you need me."

"He's not Mr. William ... he's Uncle Bill!" said Wilhelmina scornfully.

"Good lord," exclaimed Mr. William, "it can talk now! It could only coo and dribble last time I saw it. Look, Sis, I'm coming with you to the airport."

Kitty shook her head. "Do you mind if I turn that down, Bill? I—don't want to keep breaking down. If I'm with you, I will. I'm better for the moment with strangers."

Mr. William looked at me, a question in his eyes. I nodded. It was true.

He said, "Serena, look after Wilhelmina for a few moments while I see my sister into the car. Kitty, is there anything—"

"You ought to know? Yes." She turned to me. "Her case is down in the car, Bill can bring it up. There's so little time to explain. She has cereal with milk and sugar in the mornings and fruit juice and occasionally the sort of porridge Bunty brought us up on—rolled oats, and vegetables and mince and fish—only take all the bones out—at lunchtime, with fruit or milk puddings, and egg or cheese or tomato dishes for her tea. Actually I've got a lot of tinned foods in her case. The sort of things you get in the States, but not always here.

"She has a sleep every afternoon and if she sleeps well doesn't go to bed till seven again. She's out of nappies, of course, through the daytime, and she's almost always dry at nights now, but I take no risks." (I could have laughed at the look on Mr. William's face.) "And—and she likes me to sing to her after she first goes to bed. And she always takes her teddy to bed with her. That rather grubby thing she's clutching."

She stopped, said, "I'd better make this snappy, I think," caught up her baby, kissed her and said : "Be a good girl with Uncle Bill and Serena, darling, you'll have lots of fun," and was gone, Mr. William with her.

When Mr. William came back, very white, he found me sitting on the floor with Wilhelmina and an upturned wastepaper basket which she was trying to fit on my head.

I saw his eyes were bright and liked him the better for that glimpse of unshed tears. He dropped on to the office carpet, picked up a handful of crumpled sheets of paper and let them cascade on to his niece's head, a bit of fun which she received with squeals of delight.

He said, "Serena, did I do right? I feel I ought to have gone with her, to be with her when that stretcher comes off the Globemaster."

I shook my head. "She'd far rather think you were with Wilhelmina ... someone of her very own. Later, when the child is settled, you could go up."

Mr. William nodded. "I'm going to ring and book her a room at the Clarendon. It's fairly near. I know she won't leave the hospital while—till Jeff's out of danger—but it would be somewhere to leave her luggage and—"

Our eyes met. There were so many "ifs."

Then Mr. William said slowly, "I'll ring the American Headquarters and get them to let me know immediately what shape he's in on arrival, and if—if anything goes wrong, I can charter a plane and fly up right away."

All of a sudden I saw his expression change as he looked at his niece. My eyes followed his.

He said in a tone of great unease, "Serena, what's the matter with her?"

I looked at him pityingly. "I rather think the lady wants the powder-room, Mr. William. I'll take her along."

"Thank heaven you're coming out to Tattoo Bluff for the weekend," said Mr. William shakily. "There's more to this child care than I'd thought." I got Wilhelmina there in the nick of time.

It was quite an afternoon. When the buyer from McGrunn and Quentin's arrived in, he had to step over dozens of blocks, a doll's pram and a plastic duck that quacked as it was dragged along by Wilhelmina, all things brought from Durbridge's toy department by her distracted uncle. Mr. McGrunn looked as if he thought we'd gone mad, and I had to type a letter for the Customs Department again because Wilhelmina had managed to bring half the bottom row of keys down on it at the one time.

By the time Wilhelmina had nearly swallowed Mr. William's fountain pen cap and while sitting on his knee had said, "Hullo, man," into the phone while he was speaking to the manager of the Otago Savings Bank, Mr. William had had it.

At a quarter to five he said, "Come on, Serena, that's all I can take in these surroundings. The shop can take care of itself till nine." (It was late-closing night.) "Thank heaven it's Saturday tomorrow. Couldn't have worked out better. Something to be said for Saturday closing after all, though my grandmother has never liked it."

(I'd heard she was a bit of a slave-driver.)

"We'll go up and get your case, Serena, and see your mother and—Wilhelmina, let go, don't pull it!"

Too late. She had reached out and grabbed the nifty little plastic gadget that contained our pins, our clips, our drawing-pins and, of all things, our gum-spots! Mr. William and I got down on our knees. Wilhelmina uttered a crow of delight and leapt on his back. "Gee-up, gee-up!" she cried, and kicked him in the ribs with great gusto. I dissolved into the giggles.

"I can only be thankful Granny isn't here!" said Mr. William. "Just imagine if she too had decided on a surprise visit and copped us like this!"

Wilhelmina reached over, grabbed a handful of my hair and tugged. It hurt. It came away from its moorings. My tortoiseshell buckle fell out of it and in two seconds I looked completely dishevelled. At that auspicious moment, Miss Buckingham, head of the haberdashery, and as prim and proper as they make them, walked in.

Mr. William slid his niece off his back by rearing up, turned to get up quickly and put his hand down flat on a number of drawing-pins that had fallen with their business ends up. He cut off what he started to say with commendable control and I managed to make Wilhelmina let go of the wet sponge she had dug out of the moistener—not without tears—and to push my hair back out of my face. As soon as I got Wilhelmina mopped up and restored to smiles, I'd twist my hair up again.

Mr. William said, laughing, "Now, Milly, don't look like that. This is Kitty's daughter, and like mother, like child, I presume."

"But surely," said Miss Buckingham acidly, "you can keep her controlled."

"Well, not here," he grinned. "Too confined a space. We're making for Tattoo Bluff. A hundred and fifty acres should do it. Miss Smith is coming out to stay with us for the weekend to help me." He dropped his voice. "Kitty's husband's been injured down in the Antarctic. He's being flown back. Kitty just arrived for the winter break to meet him—and was greeted by news like that. She came down on one plane and went back by the next, having dumped Wilhelmina on me. As you know, Bunty still has her foot in plaster, so Serena has come to the rescue."

I felt slightly dismayed. I'd have thought Mr. William would have been more discreet. I was most amazed to see the glint of a tear in Miss Buckingham's eye. "Poor Kitty! It's not all honey being married to these adventurous men, is it, Mr. William?"

She unbent to the extent of bending down and ruffling Wilhelmina's hair, asked a few questions re Jeff's injuries—of which Mr. William knew very little in any case—and departed.

I looked at Mr. William. "Was it wise to tell her I'm going out to Tattoo Bluff for the weekend?"

"Oh, rubbish, girl. Miss Buckingham knows Bunty

well. She'll know there's no chance of any funny business going on under *her* eagle eye!"

I turned pink. "Mr. William, I didn't mean that. I just meant it's hardly wise for a man's name to be coupled in any way with his secretary's. Any shop is a hotbed of gossip."

"That's why it's much better to be quite open. My sister is in a spot of trouble... naturally she rushed home with her daughter, and as I haven't a wife to help out and Bunty can't even bend at the moment, my secretary is helping out. Or has she regretted her rash but warmhearted impulse?

"And I never am sure what you mean, Serena. It's about time you learned to let yourself go. Time you got over all these inhibitions you developed because of suspicious former bosses' wives and mothers! *I'm* as free as air, make my own decisions... my own relationships. Even Granny is at the other side of the Pacific, praise be! I ought to have asked Kitty if she's seen Gran lately, though Gran is in Texas. Beats me why she's stayed so long in one state." His voice dropped a little. "Serena, I really need you. If it should just happen that Jeff should want to see his daughter—I mean if things go wrong and he wants a last glimpse— I'll need you right on the spot to go up on the plane with us. A man is somewhat handicapped for escorting small damsels of two and a bit."

I felt ashamed. I looked down, then up. "I'm sorry, Mr. William. That was very self-centred of me... thinking about what people might say. I ought to say— want to say—that I do admire you for taking Wilhelmina on for the weekend, a single man."

"Good. I do myself. Now, let's be perfectly natural with each other. I think Wilhelmina will need us that way. Children sense atmosphere quickly. Would you just forget I'm your employer for the weekend? That's what rattles you, isn't it? You feel it's not good policy out of working hours. Well, from the moment we step out of this building, my dear Serena, I'm not your boss. I say, what's your mother going to say?"

I couldn't help it. I grinned back. "I've no doubt at

all, Mr. William, that you'll be able to twist her round
your little finger!"

Mother was so solidly approving of my going out to
Tattoo Bluff that I began to wonder why I myself had
had misgivings. "I'm so glad you volunteered, Serena.
I'd have been ashamed of you if you hadn't, poor mite.
But what a blessing she's too young to know much."

She turned to Mr. William. "I'm sorry I can't come
to help you, but you've got Bunty for moral support.
I'm taking place in a panel discussion tonight at the
Ministers' Wives meeting and it so happens my husband has made an appointment for both of us to meet
with a young couple whose marriage is on the rocks,
tomorrow morning, and we have a wedding at six.
However, I'm sure you'll manage all right. Serena has
a magic touch with Douglas's children, Judy and
Warwick. By the way, how is Bunty, Bill?"

Bill!

Really, Mother was the limit! He was, after all, my
boss. He ought to have been Mr. Durbridge to her.
And she'd said once she could never think of him as
other than Mr. William, because I invariably called
him that. They must have got on famously the other
night. I wondered uneasily what they had talked about.

Mother caught my expression and said, "It's all
right, Serena, he asked me to call him Bill, and after
all he's just Douglas's age." She added : "And Bill's my
favourite name. I always wanted a son called Bill. We
called Douglas after my father-in-law, of course. I
started off planning two sons and two daughters. Then
for long enough it looked as if our family had stopped
at three. Debbie was a surprise."

I hurriedly changed the subject. Mother wasn't
exactly naïve, but she was inclined to speak her
thoughts, which was at times disconcerting.

She took Wilhelmina off my hands while I packed.
She always had a box of toys in the bottom of her
wardrobe for the children of parishioners who came
to visit.

"Makes the mothers more easy and the children

happy," she confided to my boss. "I remember how I used to hate visiting with the children when they were small, always on tenterhooks for fear they got into mischief out of sheer boredom. Especially Serena, who was such a tomboy and so meddlesome." I went off.

When I came back Wilhelmina was contentedly fitting aluminium pill-boxes together and Mother and Mr. William were chatting ninety to the dozen. Mother picked up Wilhelmina, Mr. William the box of toys, and I carried my case.

Bunty was upset about Jeff, her face puckered and her lip trembled, but she was delighted to have Wilhelmina. Children had made her world, you could see that.

"Let's just make up our minds that Jeff will be restored and that he'll be able to convalesce down here. It will do Kitty good to spend a few weeks in her own country. I know they've been good to her in America, but she must sometimes get homesick for us."

"And us for her," said Mr. William quietly.

An unaccustomed tinge of pity stirred me for him, for this self-sufficient—seeming—boss of mine.

At first, having seen him so often in the company of the glamorous Veronica, I'd thought of him solely as a butterfly type, living for pleasure, but what sort of life was it really?

His parents, apparently, lived mainly in Europe. His sister was in the States. Even his formidable grandmother was there this year.

But Wilhelmina gave us no time for reflections.

Bunty said : "There'll never be a dull moment with that child in the house. My, but she reminds me of you, when you were small, Bill. Look at her . . . just full of deviltry !"

Yes, and brimming over with animal spirits. Nevertheless, the fact that she was such a handful gave us little time for worrying over Jeff, and she certainly didn't fret for her mother.

Every now and then I had a queer feeling. Was this

really me, in Mr. William's house, with Wilhelmina sitting between us for tea and demanding that each of us hold one of her hands, while she said grace? Bunty, in a chair by the fire, with her leg stiffly propped on a hassock, nodded approvingly.

"Well, Kitty's brought her daughter up in the right way, despite living in the States."

Mr. William burst out laughing. "Bunty thinks living in the States is all done in the style of Hollywood. She looks for signs of dissipation every time poor Kitty comes home."

"I do not, then, Mr. William. That's enough of your nonsense."

Wilhelmina said clearly: "Wirramina likes pepper on her egg. Lots and lots of pepper."

Mr. William said: "Little girls your age can't possibly have pepper."

I gave him a kick under the table, picked up the pepper-pot and, unnoticed by Wilhelmina, put my finger over the holes and shook it vigorously over the egg. He looked at me with the greatest respect. "Where did you learn all this cupidity?"

"From my niece and nephew, to say nothing of Mother. My mother is a wizard at dodging issues. The trouble she's averted through managing children without raising defiance by saying a straight-out no, you just wouldn't believe."

Mr. William exchanged glances with Bunty. "You and Mrs. Smith will have a lot in common, Bunty. She evidently follows your line of the iron hand in the foam rubber glove. And tell me, Serena, does she also really put her foot down when needed?"

"She does. There's a certain tone in Mother's voice that tells us when we've gone far enough."

Bunty clucked approvingly. "That's the best kind of discipline. Much more effective than ranting and raving. Plus, of course, the occasional spank on the place where the good Lord meant us to spank . . . and never with anything more than your own hand, so you know when you're spanking too hard."

Mrs. Hayle did the dishes while we got Wilhelmina

to bed, after a long session of romping, during which we, coached by Wilhelmina, performed round and round, squatting, quacking like ducks, crowing like roosters, gobbling like turkeys and grunting like pigs.

I say *we* got her to bed, because she even demanded Uncle Bill attend the bathing rites so he could see how well she could swim. Which she pronounced as "fwim."

I felt rather self-conscious sitting on the bed singing to her, till Mr. William joined in. I think he knew. Wilhelmina demanded a long repertoire. I was quite certain she didn't have as many songs each night as this, but we felt so desolated at the thought of her daddy winging back across those icy waters, still and unheeding, that we didn't mind the time spent.

We finished up with "Jesus, Tender Shepherd, hear me, Bless Thy little lamb tonight..." Then Wilhelmina knelt up in bed, put her chubby hands together (they had a dimple at the root of each finger) and said a marathon prayer, evidently for most people in the United States of America, beginning with the President.

Mr. William appeared to be on high priority, because "Uncle Bill" came right after Mummy and Daddy, and before two sets of grandparents. When she had finished, she shot her eyes open, pointed at me and said: "... an' her!" and shut her eyes again, screwing them up in that tight-lidded fashion of children that I find so endearing. Then she snuggled down on her pillow, cuddled Teddy under her chin, and thankfully we departed.

As we went downstairs Mr. William said: "Phew! Thank goodness that's over. I feel completely exhausted. I'd never dreamed parenthood could be so demanding."

I said severely, "It's extremely good for you. Bachelors simply have no idea how much work children are."

At that moment we heard it, a very heavy droning. We both stopped dead on the landing, listening.

You could always distinguish the big planes that came up from Antarctica, from the Friendships and

Viscounts that flew so regularly from Dunedin to Christchurch and North Island airports.

Mr. William's face suddenly looked drawn and much older.

He turned and opened the double lattice. We leaned out together.

The lamps of the sky were shining brightly in cloud-free heavens . . . and there, over the dark sea, was a red tail-light moving north. Our very stillness was a shared prayer. Jeff was on his way to Kitty. Still alive, we hoped.

Instinctively I moved nearer Mr. William. His left arm came round my shoulders. I didn't move away.

We watched the Globemaster's progress till long after it had gone out of our vision, our eyes straining after it in the darkness.

For one heavenly moment Mr. William put his cheek, slightly rough, against mine. "Thanks for just being here, Serena," he said, and before he released me, turned his face and kissed me very lightly on my cheek.

I didn't trust him with his Mollys and Veronicas, but oh, how I liked him. How achingly, how burningly, I wanted him. He hadn't turned to Veronica for help. Oh, well, what man would? Veronica was a good-time girl, fascinating, ruthless, hard as nails.

And Molly was an unknown quantity.

This situation was not of my seeking, but it would be something to remember. I didn't want the type of man in my life who could be so indiscriminating as to fall for anyone as artificial and phoney as Veronica Boleyn. I wanted someone steady and constant. I wanted the sort of married life Mother had had, with never a tremor of fear that Father might fancy some-one else. With all the irksome duties that fell to the lot of a minister's wife, the drain on her time, the some-times petty demands, she had that glorious compensa-tion . . . security in loving.

Hayley had coffee waiting for us. Surprisingly, Bunty said she was going to bed and would have hers up there. "I'm very tired tonight and after a short read

I'll drop off to sleep. I hope that child sleeps and doesn't disturb the pair of you."

Mr. William and Hayley helped Bunty upstairs. Then Mrs. Hayle went off to her own place and Mr. William joined me.

"Do you want T.V., Serena?" he asked. "Or—" He stopped.

"Or what, Mr. William?"

He gave a deprecating sort of grin. "I was going to ask you if you would like to do a crossword. Doesn't sound exciting, though, does it?"

"I love them. As a family we're addicted to them."

Mr. William sprang up, moved round the room selecting books, the Oxford Companion to English Literature, a book of quotations, a dictionary, a book of synonyms, Pears' Encyclopaedia and an atlas, then brought them over. He pulled a big chintzy couch nearer the fire.

"Come on, Serena, let's get at it."

It was most domestic. It lulled all my instinctive dislike of him. It also set my pulses beating a little— just a little—more quickly, which made me cross with myself.

Our shoulders touched. I had the most ridiculous impulse to turn and bury my head on his shoulder. I knew I mustn't. I was simply helping out.

The phone rang. It was on a cane table close against the couch at my side. I was so used to answering Mr. William's calls I automatically reached out a hand, but he leapt up. "I'd better take that, Serena."

I realised why, instantly. It could be Veronica. And Veronica wasn't the sort to think I was necessary to look after his niece. It would take some explaining. She would think Wilhelmina could have been parked at Hayley's. Just as well a ring had come. It served to remind me that my employer was a gay lad, not my type.

Mr. William said : "Oh, it's your mother, Serena. I'll have a word with her first. Yes, she's settled beautifully, thanks, Catherine." (*Catherine*!) "We've been up to her twice, but she's not stirred since she dropped off.

No, we've not heard from Kitty yet, but the plane was late. It's not long since we heard it go up. But she's bound to ring me tonight—or if she can't leave Jeff, someone from Headquarters will. Yes, I'll ring you when we hear—unless it's too late. Oh, all right, if it will set your mind at rest I'll ring whatever time we hear. Okay, I do appreciate that. Do you want to speak to Serena? No? Well, cheerio for now, Catherine."

Mother didn't want to speak to *me*. She was quite happy to have spoken to Mr. William. Mother always vowed she wasn't a matchmaker, that all she did was work for people's happiness ... something that made Father laugh derisively. And she had taken to Mr. William. I'd have to disillusion her, tell her I didn't care for the type of woman he ran round with.

Mr. William said: "I'd like to have taken you to see the moon rise up from the sea—from Tattoo Bluff—it's a glorious night. But Bunty couldn't get out of bed quickly to attend Wilhelmina if she called, and also I'd like to be at hand when Kitty rings."

"Of course," I said quickly. "Anyway, I'm not sold on the idea. Moons can be overrated. I'd sooner do a crossword."

Mr. William took my chin, forced it round, and looked deeply into my eyes. "You try too hard to be a common-sense girl, Serena. Why? It's no more natural than your fawn-coloured hair. Why, I'm asking you?"

I couldn't hold his eyes. So I said, looking down, "I find this stupid and embarrassing."

"Why stupid?"

I looked up, tried to appear cool and amused. "Men seem to think that a moon and *any* company ought to add up to romance. If a girl is sensible she doesn't go moon-watching with just *anyone*. If she appears ready to, then she could be accused of encouraging him."

Two lines appeared between his brows, then they smoothed out and he laughed. "Now, you'll probably accuse me of being vain, but I don't care. I've an idea you could quite easily enjoy moon-watching with *me*. We *suit*."

This time I managed to gaze at him levelly, giving

away nothing in my expression. "*I* think I only intrigue you because I've tried—till now—to brush you off. Mr. William, I'm only here to help with your little niece, in an emergency. I rather thought Bunty would be with us this evening. You led me to believe so when you mentioned Bunty and Hayley as duennas. I think we'd better watch television . . . in separate chairs."

It was the first time I'd ever seen Mr. William really angry—which is something not everyone can say of their boss.

He actually went white. "Serena! That was uncalled for. You don't really think for a moment that I'd take advantage of you being here tonight, do you? If so, let me tell you, you've formed a very wrong idea of me. No matter how much I might want to hold you, to kiss you, I'd never do it against your will."

I found that I was breathing hard, that I didn't know where to go from here, what to say, and I had to fight the maddest impulse to throw myself in his arms.

I finally managed, shakily, "Mr. William, I'm sorry . . . I didn't mean to suggest you would—" I stopped, took a deep breath, added, "Oh, I don't know how all this sprang up. Let's forget it. I'd no right to be so prickly when you're so upset about your brother-in-law."

His voice was scathing, not forgiving. "Oh, I claim no advantages, Serena. Don't put a strain on yourself trying to understand me."

I bit my lip. "I'm afraid we just strike sparks off each other, Mr. William. Look, let's forget this, please? Let's go back to a quietly friendly footing. I mean it's necessary for this weekend for Wilhelmina's sake. I—I just hate myself for upsetting you." I picked up the crossword book lying between us. "Let's go on with this."

He shook his head. "No, you've ruined the atmosphere for that—or perhaps I did, bringing in the moon. We'll watch television. In separate chairs."

He went across, switched on the set, then crossed to turn out the centre light, leaving just the standard lamp behind us.

He snorted. "And I'm not turning out this light for a setting for romance, either! Merely for better viewing, so no more dirty cracks from you."

He crossed to a chair nearer the fire, took out his pipe, began cramming tobacco in. I felt like nothing on earth.

I don't remember one single thing about that programme. Just as it ended the phone rang.

It was obvious from the short wait it was a toll call. Then he said, "Kitty darling, how is he?"

Then, heavily, "Not conscious yet? How bad is the damage? No, of course they can't tell till the X-rays are through. Kitty, I hate like hell to think of you waiting there alone . . . but just think we're here thinking of you and praying for you. Listen, Kit, Wilhelmina has settled beautifully with us. Serena, I know, would stay with her tomorrow and let me away to fly up by the first plane. I can come back late in the day if you feel happier. No, Serena won't mind. I have a gem of a secretary, Sis, she rises to any occasion."

I was sure his eyes, over the instrument, were mocking me.

He rang Mother, told her the report, and what he proposed doing. Mother approved. I had a feeling she would approve everything he ever proposed.

He rang the airways and got a seat on the first plane, then he said, resuming his seat, "I'll take the car to Momona and leave it in the car-park. Even if I don't get back till Sunday night it won't matter. You can cope with Wilhelmina, can't you?"

I said of course I could and he switched the sound on again.

Odd how tension can disappear under the influence of a good programme. I could remember Mother saying once that if only quarrelling husbands and wives would take themselves off to a happy-ending film, they'd find it hard to go on with the fight afterwards.

But if only I could be a little more hard-boiled. If only I could think it's only fiction. But I can't. I live every moment of such things. It got very poignant. I swallowed, quite audibly. I tried to sniff silently. It's impossible. So very surreptitiously I tried to extricate my handkerchief from my sleeve—but the darned thing wasn't there!

Suddenly Mr. William crossed over, dropped down on the couch beside me, and thrust his handkerchief at me. "Goose!" he said. "Don't be so afraid of showing emotion."

He said nothing more than that, and when it came to an end, the end I—we had hoped for, we sat for a few moments in perfect silence. I say perfect because it *was* just that, and I realised that very few men of my acquaintance would have sat like this...they'd have been flippant about it, perhaps scornful of the sentiment.

Then Mr. William got up, switched off, said, "Very satisfying. Now I'll make us some supper. It will be an early start."

So as soon as we had drunk our tea and eaten our biscuits, we started upstairs. By mutual but unspoken consent we tiptoed into Wilhelmina's room. In case she felt strange if she woke, we had left a small reading lamp on the bureau, with its shade throwing the light away from her face, but there was just enough light from it to see the bright hair spread across the pillow, the shadow fan of her lashes on her cheeks. One little hand was flung out.

Mr. William lifted it gently, tucked it beneath the bedclothes. She did not stir. From opposite sides of the bed our eyes met, held, smiled.

Then I stole to the door, Mr. William followed me. My room was next to Wilhelmina's. Mr. William opened my door, put his hand to the switch, but stayed there without pulling it down. A shaft of the moonlight I had spurned earlier shone down on us from the landing skylight.

We turned and looked at each other.

I still don't know who moved first. But suddenly we were very near and both of us were breathing hard. Mr. William's hands came out to my wrists, touched them lightly, then I felt them against my shoulder-blades, urging me towards him.

His eyes smiled down into mine. I knew I ought to push him away and reject this moment, but I couldn't. I felt powerless. That if I did reject it, I would regret it all my life.

Then his lips came down on mine. Oh, I'd been kissed before. I'd even been kissed more passionately. But never like this.

I knew it wouldn't mean as much to him—couldn't. But never had a kiss stirred me so . . . the sweetness of it running like a spring tide through my veins. Something I would remember when I was eighty, and grow young again. . . .

I still felt bemused when we drew apart.

Mr. William was smiling. "You said we struck sparks off each other. We do, don't we? In the nicest possible way. I think it ends our arguing, doesn't it, Serena? I said I wouldn't do it against your will, and I didn't . . . did I?"

Fortunately he didn't force me to answer him. I was beyond words, and anyway, everything he said was absolutely true.

He laughed. I thought it was an exultant laugh, yet strangely I didn't resent that exultancy. "I daresay forced kisses could have a flavour all their own, but that was quite perfect, Serena. A kiss given and shared, not just taken. Goodnight."

My own goodnight to him was just a shred of sound. As I drifted off to sleep I was still thinking about that kiss. Certainly there were kisses *and* kisses. Some didn't mean a thing. A salute, a touch of lips on lips, something purely local. This hadn't been like that. It had been something that had seemed to take possession of all of me. Something I had never experienced before.

I was going to have to revise my ideas of Mr. William. I could see that. Certainly he'd been rushing Veronica Boleyn these past few weeks—even months— but perhaps it had been that he'd been more serious about me and taken my refusals to go out with him more to heart than I had imagined and it had sprung up out of that. Anyway, even flirts settled down . . . Smiling, I fell asleep. . . .

CHAPTER SIX

COMMON sense ought to have returned in the cold, hard light of day, but it didn't.

When I woke I still felt caught up in remembered magic. I could hear someone moving about, very quietly, downstairs. Mr. William had been adamant last night that Hayley was not to get up to get his breakfast.

"You know perfectly well you always have a sleep-in on Sundays. I'd not have let you know I was going up if I'd thought you would insist on that," he had said when he phoned their cottage to tell them how Jeff was. "It's a feeble sort of chap who can't rustle up a plate of bacon and eggs and a jorum of tea. If you arrive over I'll throw you out, Hayley."

Maybe those things had added up to my lessened distrusts of him . . . a man I'd deemed to be a flirt, a breaker of hearts. His affection for Bunty and Hayley, for all the things I knew of him from the shop—the way he sometimes visibly controlled his temper when some of the die-hard heads of departments drove him to distraction; the way he ironed out tensions; his incredible ability to remember the names of even the most junior members of staff.

I got up, seized my dressing-gown, glad it wasn't too glamorous, peeped in on Wilhelmina to find her still asleep (though goodness knew how long it would last) and crept downstairs.

Mr. William had a frying-pan on the stove and was pouring orange juice into a glass. He swung round and smiled in a way that lit his eyes up and made my heart skip a beat.

I said deprecatingly, "I'm not even washed . . . but I didn't want to wake Wilhelmina with the sound of running water. I thought I ought to help you get away. Have you got your bag packed in case you stay the night? I mean if—if Kitty needed you."

We both knew what I really meant . . . if Jeff was so

critically injured that her brother needed to stay to
see Kitty through her darkest hour.

"Could you cope with Wilhelmina the whole time
if I did, Serena?"

"Of course. It might have seemed exhausting to you
yesterday because you aren't used to tiny tots, but I'm
so accustomed to my niece and nephew."

"Right, bless you. If you like to watch this pan I'll
go and clean my shoes. Have some with me, won't
you?"

He cleaned them outside the kitchen door on a bench
that looked as if it had been used for that purpose for
three or four generations.

I had the tea made and the bacon and eggs ready
to serve when he came in. I said, "I've buttered your
toast for you and cut it into fingers because I don't feel
you've any too much time and I didn't want you
speeding."

His well-cut mouth twitched. "You sound exactly
like my grandmamma, Serena. But how nice of you to
be concerned."

I said hastily : "Oh, I'm given to thinking things
like that when *anyone* goes away. Is it any wonder,
considering the death-toll on the roads?"

"No, it isn't." The sherry-brown eyes were dancing
with fun. "You sure do cut me down to size, Serena,
don't you? You make sure I don't get above myself . . .
just like Bunty. Why?"

I got all confused. "I don't know what you mean.
Mr. William, you haven't time to do anything else but
eat."

"I can talk beautifully with my mouth full," he said.
"I've had a lot of practice. Is there any need—still—
to be so on the defensive with me, after last night?"

I could feel my colour rising. Mr. William laughed
teasingly but didn't—mercifully—press for an answer.

We finished, gulping down the last of our tea. He
rose and held out a hand to me. "Come and see me
off . . . just to the stable gate."

Had there ever been such a beautiful morning? The
view of the sea from Blueskin Bay was just one shim-

mering sheet of palest blue with the sun already well up from the Pacific horizon, the light gleaming on countless seabirds' wings and on the white tower of the light on Taiaroa Head.

From across the beaten-hard, dry white ground of the approach to the stables, the breath, aromatic and powerful, of Australian blue-gums came to us, and over to the left a group of ribbonwoods showed a bridal transparency of blossom cups that made one think for an enchanted moment that it was spring, not autumn.

Geraniums blazed against the white stone of the house, the flowerbeds were blooming in that riot of fragrance and colour that is so much more aggressive than the summer blooming, a last mad resistance against the coming winter.

Some of the Tattoo Bluff paddocks were already stubble-fields, but beyond the ribbonwoods was a meadow of nothing but red clover. Even from here you could hear the happy sound of bees. A lovely, lovely world.

A singing happiness pervaded my heart. I felt as if I were teetering on the brink of new, warm, breathless adventures.

Would Mr. William kiss me goodbye? If he did, would I find that same magic? Would it mean a sort of confirmation of the unexpected, of that wild sweet hoping that had sprung up in my heart last night and had lasted right through my dreams? A conviction that Mr. William was not the lightweight he had appeared, not the flirt. That something—me—had changed him.

Mr. William went straight into the open part of the stable he used as a garage, threw his small case in, got in the driving seat, backed out, turned and came to a stop beside me.

The sunlight shone on his brown hair. The brown eyes met mine. I knew he wasn't going to get out and kiss me goodbye. And it didn't matter. This interchanged look was a caress in itself.

He smiled. "I'm not going to kiss you goodbye,

Serena. I don't want anything hurried to overlay what happened to us last night."

That was perfection. I had my back to the sun so that wasn't what was dazzling my eyes.

He leaned out, said softly, "And I would appreciate your prayers today, Serena."

I didn't dare step up close to him. I just held out my hand. He reached out as far as he could and squeezed the tips of my fingers.

I said softly, "You didn't really need to ask for them, did you, Mr. William?"

"No. Goodbye, Serena. Take care of yourself. And you'd better start thinking of me as Bill while I'm away."

The dust spurted up, just like in a Western. What an odd thing to think in a moment like this. I stood there watching while the Chevrolet disappeared down the first gully, reappeared briefly on the crest of the next hill, then was gone from my sight. I picked up my long skirts and ran happily into the house and up to Wilhelmina.

He rang us up at four-thirty. "Serena, there's a ray of hope. He regained consciousness very briefly and has lapsed again now, but isn't so deep. His pulse is stronger. The first thing he saw was Kitty's face. He was reassured when he found I was there—for Kitty's sake. We said to him that Wilhelmina was at Tattoo Bluff with Bunty and that his mother was on her way across the Pacific. She's flying out with some personnel for the base. Kitty sent her word just before Jeff's plane touched down."

I said: "We heard on the news that he had been safely landed and transferred to Christchurch Hospital, but that his condition was unchanged then. I'm so glad he's had even that brief moment of recognition. I'll let Bunty and Hayley know. Wilhelmina is taking our mind off the waiting for news. Tell Kitty she's having a wonderful time. This is the right spot for her. She loves animals. And we've got all Kitty's dolls out on the playroom floor—plus your old trains and cars—and I've had fifteen miniature cups of tea out of that lovely tea-set. Bunty and Hayley are completely fascinated with her."

"Thank you, Serena, that's what Kitty will want to hear, even if, at the moment, ninety-nine per cent of her is Jeff's."

I said, though I longed to keep him talking, "Mr. William, you mustn't stay. Get right back to Kitty. These sort of vigils are only bearable if you have some-one with you."

"That's true, but how did you know, Serena?"

"Long experience of manse life, Mr. William. In manse life you are always close to the big moments . . . christenings and marriages and deaths. Goodbye for now, Mr. William."

"Goodbye, Serena. You evidently haven't been mentally practising it. Saying Bill, I mean. I'll keep in touch."

I tried to say it over and over to myself. Bill, Bill, Bill. It didn't register. When I said Bill I couldn't summon up the image of his face in front of me. As soon as I whispered Mr. William, I could see those teasing, mobile eyebrows, the well-cut mouth, the light in the sherry-brown eyes. Even the way the smooth brown hair swept sideways.

He rang again at eight that night. "Jeff's had quite a few periods of consciousness. They're operating tomorrow morning. They think the damage may not be as serious as at first feared. Kitty, I'm afraid, is still very frozen, holding herself as taut as a violin string, almost as if she were willing him to get better through sheer concentration on it. I won't leave her, of course. We're allowed to stay at the hospital meantime.

"I'll stay till he's out of danger, Serena. I certainly won't leave until at least the third day after the opera-tion. His mother will be here then. The shop will just have to get on without you and me. Can you stay with Wilhelmina? I think it would set Kitty's mind at rest. Just once in a while she tears her mind away from Jeff and says things like : 'Serena wouldn't let her take the path to the sea, would she, Bill?' Or, 'Serena will watch she doesn't pull pans over on herself, won't she, Bill?' I assured her you'd said to me one had to have eyes in the back of one's head. That Hayley had brought in our old fireguard and that I'd noticed you put cold water in her bath first. I thought of a few things myself, Serena. Not to let her in the paddock with the horses. And to keep the lower windows of the upstairs rooms shut."

I promised him I'd watch Wilhelmina like a hawk. He went on to give me detailed instructions for office procedure and I took them down and said I'd ring them through first thing Monday morning. There were appointments with travellers to be cancelled or else handled by the buyers, and others to be indefinitely postponed.

Then he said he'd like to speak to Bunty. Hayley was back in the cottage, so he just sent her his love. "But don't get Bunty yet, Serena. I didn't mean right away."

I said, heart beating fast, foolishly, "Have you remembered something else about the office, Mr. William?"

"No, I have not, Miss Smith! But it's to do with remembering, just the same. Listen, Serena . . . I'm ringing from a hospital phone. I don't want to be at any distance from Kitty yet. So there are things I can't say. You'll know what I mean. I'll just say : Don't let things fade."

I'm sure he must have heard me swallowing at the other end.

He laughed. "Cat got your tongue, Serena?"

I said hastily : "B-Bunty's right here in the room, Mr. William."

He laughed again. "I get it. You're in the same spot of bother I'm in. Not that it would matter. Bunty's very astute. She's probably already seen how it is with us. But never mind . . . I'll just imagine the sort of things you'd say if you were alone. May I?"

I gulped again. "I—I don't know."

He chuckled. "Perhaps not the answer—quite—I was hoping for, but it will do meantime. It's something to know I've disturbed my Serene Miss Smith enough to get her all confused. But I'm sure it's charming con-fusion. All right, Serena, I won't tease any longer. Put me on to Bunty."

Little wonder I went to bed in a daze of happiness, coming out of it now and then to feel absolutely reproached that I could be so ecstatic when Kitty was so heartbreakingly sad. But then life was like that.

I remembered Dad saying once how he'd had to pull into a side road at Mother's request when they were en route from the cemetery to a wedding. It had been the funeral of a treasured child. It had taken Dad all his time to get control of himself too, but they had some-how managed it because while they had to weep with those who wept, they had also to rejoice with those who rejoiced, and they wanted no shadow to fall on that wedding feast.

So I stopped whipping myself for feeling happy. I hadn't known that this sweet sense of possessing and being possessed was what being in love meant. I knew now, of course, that I'd been in love with Mr. William for months. But I'd been too tied up inside to face it.

I had been terrified of getting involved again, in a personal way, with an employer, something I knew could lead to losing one's job. I had distrusted the effect my looks had on men. I felt I always attracted the wrong sort, the sort that fell in love with outward things, surface beauty. That no one was going to fall in love with the real me, the inner me, who was tom-boyish and home-loving and so very ordinary. That if I marrried someone who fell in love with my looks, it wouldn't last if my looks faded, if illness came along, if the years dimmed my colouring.

I surveyed my mouse-coloured hair with sheer affec-tion. It had paid off.

I kept going over and over everything that had happened since I had met Mr. William. I'd have to get round to calling him Bill. I really had been severe with him from the start, refusing to lunch with him, being cold and distant with him, even rude in dis-couraging his advances. Even his jokes I had merely indulged with a frosty smile, unwilling to let the barriers down.

No wonder he'd started running that Veronica around. I instantly quelled the deep unease that stirred as I thought of her . . . it was really my own fault. Veronica had been handy, ready to accept Mr. William as he was. It must have been balm to him after my rebuffs. I tortured myself by going over every pang I'd suffered when she'd rung up, when she'd breezed into the office. That time he had told me to go down to the showroom and dispatch her that exquisite white stole . . . the flowers he'd sent so often.

A comforting thought struck me. Had he been trying to make me jealous? All unquiet thoughts departed. I must not rush things. I must not want to know all the answers at once. I must cling to the reality of what we had shared, there in the doorway of my room, when all uncertainties had been stilled. I was building a whole future on it. That and what Mr. William had said on the phone: ". . . There are things I can't say . . . you'll know what I mean . . . don't let things fade." Yes, and "I'll just imagine the sort of things you'd say if you were alone . . . may I?" . . . and best of all to remember: "Bunty has probably already seen how it is with us."

How it is with us.

My pulses began to throb again. I was glad that never till now had I fallen in love. What a pity it would have been to have fallen in love as a teenager. Because now I had more to bring to my loving. And even if teenage love lasted, as it sometimes did, how hard it must be to wait so long for fulfilment.

Whereas at our age . . . I was twenty-three and someone had once said Mr. William was twenty-nine . . . we wouldn't have to wait. I'd let my hair go back to its original colour before the wedding. By then I'd have met this teacher Patsy was crazy about. Anyway, a chap wouldn't be likely to fall for a sister-in-law-to-be who was already affianced to someone else.

I pulled myself up with a jerk. I mustn't! I mustn't let my imagination go rioting. Perhaps I was reading too much into one kiss, into the look in those sherry-brown eyes as he was driving away, into a few guarded phrases uttered on the phone from two hundred miles away.

And so I spent the next few days ... between ecstasy and doubt.

Our moments on the phone were always brief. Sometimes Kitty was in the room with Mr. William when he rang, ready to speak to me about Wilhelmina. Mostly Bunty was with me. Never once were both blessedly alone. Yet I felt it was all there, in undertones, in his voice to me and in my voice to him.

The operation was successful, the damage not as severe as at first suspected. Jeff's constitution was marvellous, they said, and he came off the seriously ill list.

I had a wonderful time at Tattoo Hills with Wilhelmina and Bunty and Hayley. Mr. Hayle was a darling too. So were the other men. Mr. William had the knack of gathering good men about him, I told myself, continuing to see life—and him—through rose-tinted spectacles.

Mother and Father gave themselves an afternoon off and drove out to see me, bringing me more clothes. They enjoyed meeting Bunty and Hayley and walking round the tracks leading into the bush. It was a magnificent property, rich with pioneer history and beautifully kept. It had begun as a whaling station in the early days and there were both wild and sad tales bound up with it, but its later years had been all pastoral.

Bunty had told me a lot about the family. I loved hearing about Mr. William as a small boy. I didn't have to encourage Bunty, she got into full spate, and neither of us felt in the least bit uncomfortable about it.

How different from the gay man of the world I'd imagined him it all sounded.

I studied the photo of his grandmamma, the owner of Durbridge's, with some misgivings. She looked a woman of steel. I knew Bunty well enough by then to say one night : "Does she rule them all with a rod of iron?"

Bunty, to my surprise, said an emphatic no. "She's hard, there's no doubt about that. And they've all got a bit of her in them. That's why sometimes they clash. But she loves them for it. She would despise them otherwise. She tried to interfere with Kitty, but Kitty put her foot down. Mrs. Durbridge didn't approve of her going off to America. She's the clannish type, you know, and wanted them all about her. She offered Jeff a position, a good position in the business.

"He was absolutely astonished that she should even think of it. He said : 'Ma'am, I just can't believe my ears. I'm a scientist. I'm not likely to be bribed with talk of shares in the firm. If Kitty loves me she'll go back with me to the States. It's a woman's duty to follow her man and that's that. If she can't take it then she's not the girl I took her for.'

"So old Mrs. Durbridge capitulated immediately, told Kitty she'd picked herself a fine man, one that would be master in his own household. She always respects anyone who can stand up to her. I'm telling you this, Serena, so you'll know. Start as you mean to end. Though you aren't the sort to buckle down to anyone. You have the wrong sort of chin for that. I think myself Mrs. Durbridge will be delighted with you."

I could feel myself turning pink, and Bunty chuckled. "I've got eyes in my head," she said.

I said hastily, "Well, one is always curious about a future employer."

Bunty said, twinkling, "Of course, of course, what else?"

I said : "And what about Mr. William's parents? Are they much in New Zealand?"

"No. Mostly England, Italy, Spain. Painting."

I nodded, looking round the walls.

"Miles—Mr. William's father—was a throwback to an artist ancestor on his father's side. Old Mrs. Durbridge knew from the start he would never enter the shop, so she concentrated on Bill."

I said, exploring, "Does he not stand up to her the

same as the others? He told me once that being here, running this with a manager and having the weekends on the farm, is all that compensates him for being in the drapery business. If his grandmother accepted his father's decision, why did Mr. William knuckle down to her?"

I had to know because if what I hoped for came to pass, if Mr. William loved me and had marriage in mind, I wanted to know if Mrs. Durbridge might have the chance to run our lives.

"He didn't knuckle down to her, Serena. He so loved his grandmother. He was the only one who saw through the hard crust to what she really was. He was the only one who sensed that the shop compensated her for all she had missed in life."

"Why, Bunty, what do you mean?" I asked.

"Just that she married a poor, spineless creature. And she was one who longed to be mastered. She has never known what it means to be cherished, protected. Merton Durbridge had let the business go. He'd let this property go too. She pulled things together at both places. He was just bone lazy. Too much money.

"To see her you'd have thought both shop and land had belonged to *her* people for generations. She was surprisingly sweet and patient with Merton. He needed her. But all she did was for her son, and he wanted to be a painter. So she accepted that. And of course Bill took after the Durbridge who came here in 1840. The land was in his blood.

"But because he loved his grandmother so much, he went into the shop. She told him he didn't have to. I overheard it. She has never discussed it with me. She's a proud woman, hard but lonely."

Mr. William rang to say he was coming home on Friday. "I'll be home at noon, Serena. I'm not going to the shop, I don't want to get involved. If it's done without me all week, it can continue to do so till Monday. I've rung Jennings to tell him I'll come home at the weekend and be at the shop at nine on Monday morning. Mrs. Ralston is here with Jeff and Kitty.

Jeff's doing well. He'll be here for some time yet, but they'll all come to the Bluff when he's convalescent. I've managed to get Kitty a motel in Riccarton. Actually they're separate houses set back in a lovely space of lawns and trees. She wants us to fly up with Wilhelmina on Saturday, stay the night and fly back Sunday. Can do? Will do? Oh, good girl! I knew you would. Serena . . . ?"

I waited, breathlessly. "Yes, Mr. William?"

"Oh, let it go till I see you. Friday night's not too far off. This is tantalising, being at the other end of a telephone cable."

I laughed and said goodbye.

Friday was a perfect day with not a breath of wind ruffling the Pacific. I loved Tattoo Bluff and Blueskin Bay. I remembered our idyllic childhood in the parish Dad had in Bay of Islands in the far North . . . the semi-tropical lushness, the mirror-calm bay, studded with islands where once, below the Treaty House at Waitangi, the great canoes had waited ready for the chiefs to come ashore to sign, in the great marquee, the pact whereby the Maori people were to be united with the English, the chiefs signing with their mark, or their tattoo markings.

Although this lacked the heat and lushness of the North, it still strongly reminded me of Bay of Islands. My earliest memories had been of bush-crowned hills reaching down into bays and headlands and the incomparable sound of the sea to hush me to sleep. I'd ask no other lullaby for my own children.

In short, I had come home. The certainty had grown upon me with every moment spent away from Mr. William.

I wasn't to know that the weather wasn't at all idyllic in other parts of New Zealand. It was a day of disruptions as far as the airports were concerned. Christchurch had fog. Then when that cleared—as we heard on the news—a storm blew up in Dunedin in striking contrast to the still perfection of the morning and closed Momona with cross-winds. Finally the plane by-passed Dunedin and the air-centre told us it would land at Invercargill one hundred and forty miles south and the passengers would be brought back by bus.

By that time I was jittery and when I heard that owing to torrential rain in West Otago, the water was over the road at Waipahi and that all traffic had to take a detour, I couldn't even settle to watch T.V.

This, evidently, was what love did to you. I remembered Mother saying once, "Love raises you to the heights and destroys your peace of mind for ever. You're always thinking something will happen to your dear one." Then she had added, laughing, "But, like Judy in Daddy-Long-Legs, I say fervently : 'But I never did care much for just plain peace, anyway!' "

I took myself to task for feeling as I did. No doubt when Mother had felt like that Father had been away at the war, when fear was justified, when dread went through all the normal business of living. Nevertheless, I couldn't control my imagination. I was certain a blizzard would blow up from the South Pole, that the runways at Invercargill would be iced over, that the plane wouldn't be able to land there either, that it wouldn't have enough fuel to return, or if it did, that Christchurch would be closed again . . . that it would get off course and run slap bang into the Southern Alps.

Then we heard it *had* landed and that passengers were on their way, and I began to wonder how long it would take them if they had to detour. And if one river was up, what about the others in this land of many waters?

Finally, the air-centre said they were not expecting them till midnight. That was Dunedin arrival time, of course. And it would take another hour out to Tattoo Bluff.

I consoled myself with the thought that at least Bunty would be in bed. Her leg had been sore today. She said how glad she was that I was here, and I knew warmth at my heart realising that she and I got on so well together. It augured well for the years ahead. I could see she had strong likes and dislikes. I hoped

she'd like me just as well with my hair blonde. I'd tell
her my reasons some time.

There was something exciting in the thought of
staying up so late to welcome Mr. William. At least
we would be alone, blessedly alone.

I caught myself up on the thought . . . don't imagine
it will necessarily be perfection, Serena! It's all right
for you, you haven't been travelling. He'll be dog-tired.
And won't want to stay up because we have to
travel again tomorrow. Things went haywire like that
sometimes.

Like when Daddy got back from the war and
Granny took us and Mother went down to Wellington
to meet him and engaged a room at a pluty hotel and
it was going to be a second honeymoon—and he
tripped on the wharf rushing to meet her and finished
up in hospital with a broken leg!

But I went on planning. I'd have hot soup in a flask,
and fingers of toast with grated cheese and chips of
bacon and the fire would be red to its heart . . . and
I'd have his slippers warming on the kerb . . . the by
now familiar surge of sweetness ran through my veins
at the thought.

The phone rang. The post office. A telegram. They
read it out.

"OWING TO HAVING LEFT CAR AT MOMONA AM STAYING
NIGHT WITH DICK CARTER AT HENLEY SO CAN PICK IT UP
TOMORROW MORNING STOP SEE YOU ABOUT TEN LOVE
BILL."

Even the "love" didn't mean a thing because it was
addressed to Bunty, not to me. Which was very wise
of Mr. William because she might have been hurt
otherwise.

He would arrive about ten. It would be a scramble
. . . an early lunch, then dashing out to Momona for
one of the early afternoon planes, I supposed. And
Bunty and Wilhelmina would be with us all the time
between arrival and lunch.

In Christchurch we'd be with Mrs. Ralston and Kitty
at the hospital and the motel. We might not be alone

till we were flying back. I schooled myself to patience.
But I felt horribly flat when finally I got to bed.

Next day it was as if the storm had never been. If
anything the sea was more blue, the hills more green . . .
the wings of the seabirds were diamond-white in the
dazzling light of the sun, and the scents of the garden
blended in one glorious whole to add enchantment to
the day.

I strained my ears for the sound of a car arriving
so I could rush out and have just one moment to ourselves, eyes meeting, hands touching.

But of course I didn't hear it. We were all in the
big old kitchen having morning tea when he arrived
in. He swung Wilhelmina up to his shoulder after he
had kissed her and looked at me. Only a glance, but
what was in it made my heart sing.

"We aren't off till two-thirty," he said, sitting down
and seizing a hot buttered scone and biting into it, "so
it won't be too rushed. Got your bag and Wilhelmina's
packed, Serena?"

I nodded, and Hayley said, "I put the roast in extra
early in case you had time for lunch. We'll have it at
eleven-thirty. That will give you time to relax for a
bit."

I said, "Would you like to go upstairs and lie down
for a bit? You must be tired."

"No fear," he said promptly. "I'm not a bit fagged.
It's too good a day to spend indoors.

Wilhelmina said : "Uncle Bill, you promised we'd
have a slide in the hay. Now, please, now?"

Bunty said quickly, "He can't go sliding in those
clothes, Wilhelmina. Look, pet, you'll be coming down
again with Daddy and Mummy when he gets better . . .
you can have all the slides you want to then."

No doubt if Wilhelmina had sounded mutinous about
it she'd not have got her own way, but she didn't say
a word. Her lip just trembled.

Her uncle grinned. "I'm all for it, Wilhelmina. I'll
change. Serena, get into some trews."

It was great fun. I realised it was impossible to have

Mr. William to myself with Wilhelmina about—and besides, now he was back, all my doubts had gone. This teetering on the brink had a magic all its own ... I was aware of a warmth within that was completely new to me. Just to meet his eyes occasionally was enough. Apparently he didn't mind a girl being a tomboy at all. In fact he seemed to expect it.

I only hoped these thin trews stood up to it, that was all. They were brown and white dog's tooth check in thin glazed cotton and I had a white woven sports shirt of Mr. William's loose over the top. Bunty had got it for me.

This was a haystack that had tumbled over some time ago when a couple of cows had got in and had eaten right into it. "They darned near lost their lives ... could have been suffocated. We just got them out in time," said Mr. William.

It sounded so different from the polished shop jargon. There was a side to Mr. William I hadn't known at all, and I liked it. Much nicer to think it wouldn't be all shop atmosphere for the rest of your life ... sales and the Christmas rush and trying to get indent orders away on time and keeping an eye on the rival stores merchandise and prices ... oh, yes, I was very sure of myself ... and him.

The stack had been built near a clump of ribbonwoods and below us the cliffs sloped down to a sea that was turquoise today. We kept climbing up the tumbleddown side and sliding down a groove from the hollow at the top. Our laughter as well as our activity tired us out, but Wilhelmina, of course, was inexhaustible.

She kept clapping her hands and shrieking: "More, more! Again ... again!"

"We'll have to pack this in in a moment," said Mr. William as I picked myself up and stood ready to receive Wilhelmina as he slid her down to me. "We'll have to have showers."

I said ruefully, "I wouldn't have time to shampoo my hair, would I? Long hair takes so long to dry. It's full of bits of hay."

"I think it would be all right with just a vigorous brush, Serena."

I was laughing. "If I don't feel a wreck!"

He said softly: "You look beautiful. It's such charming disarray. Do you know Herrick's poetry, Serena?"

I blinked. "I know one about daffodils."

He shook his head. "I'm thinking of one that starts: 'A sweet disorder in the dress . . . and finishes:

'A winning wave, deserving note,
In the tempestuous petticoat—
A careless shoestring, in whose tie
I see a wild civility—
Do more bewitch me, than when art
Is too precise in every part.' "

I caught my breath with the sweetness of that. How marvellous to love a man who could quote poetry like that, entirely without embarrassment. My cup overflowed.

He said, "All right, all right, Wilhelmina. Bring her up for the last slide, Serena. We'll make it a good one and all go down together. And no grizzling, Wilhelmina. Definitely the last."

We arranged ourselves as if we were tobogganing. Wilhelmina was in front and Mr. William last, his arms clasped round me. His face was over my shoulder, his cheek faintly rough against mine. He shoved off. We came unstuck halfway down. Wilhelmina and I managed to stay together, but Mr. William slewed off sideways and somersaulted and finally crashed back on to us.

As I sat up and pushed him off, slightly winded, he laughed, swooped, and kissed me.

I pushed at his chest, said: "Not in front of Wilhelmina, you idiot!" And a thin, acidy voice from the clump of ribbonwood trees said: "And not in front of *me*, either!"

Mr. William let me go so suddenly I tipped over on the hay. I righted myself, still sitting, and stared.

A very tiny lady. Very elegant, very shocked and very angry!

It didn't need Mr. William's horrified : "Granny !" to tell me who it was.

I just couldn't believe I'd got myself into such a situation. Although my past was sprinkled with adventures like this, I'd been so circumspect since coming to Dunedin, I just couldn't believe it. I felt exactly like a maid in the Elizabethan age, caught tumbling in the hay with the groom. It was *so* awful, I giggled.

Then Mr. William broke up. Great guffaws of laughter. Wilhelmina joined in. She'd no idea what it was all about, the lamb, but like all tiny children, if grown-ups were laughing, she laughed too.

Then we stopped laughing and into the silence Mrs. Durbridge's voice said : "I am not amused."

CHAPTER SEVEN

MR. WILLIAM scrambled to his feet, gave another helpless guffaw, caught her in his arms and said, "You priceless old anachronism ... you sound exactly like Queen Victoria of blessed memory !"

She said, every word like a chip of ice falling into an aluminium shaker, "I heard you were getting involved with someone. That's why I came home."

We both stared.

I was thinking despairingly : "It's happened *again*. One wife, one mother, now a grandmother. All thinking me a menace !" But never before had it had the power to hurt me like this.

Mrs. Durbridge added as if she had to cross the t's and dot the i's for us, as we didn't seem to be taking it in. "That Mildred Banks wrote and said you were running round with a brassy blonde."

She sort of bit off the last words as if she realised something was wrong and gazed in a bewildered fashion at my mousy locks which, instead of being smoothly coiled, were half hanging round my shoulders, and indescribably spiky with hay.

Mr. William gave way to mirth again, made a determined effort to sober up and said : "You've got it all wrong, Granny darling. *That* was Veronica. *She* was a synthetic blonde. This one is a true one."

No wonder his grandmother looked foxed. She snapped back : "You must be off your head, William. This one's no colour at all. Mousy."

Mr. William said, "She dyed it mouse. I've been told on the best authority that it's really Scandinavian gold."

Her voice was impatient. "William, I may be old, but I am not daft. Girls don't dye their hair *mouse*."

"Most don't, Gran, but this girl is the exception to every rule I've ever known."

"Why would she?" Every word was snapped off short. I might just as well not have been there.

Mr. William said soberly, "It's a long story, Gran— she got sick of men paying her attention, so she took protective colouring."

I've never seen such a look on any woman's face. "Well, it doesn't seem to have succeeded, does it?"

He tried again. "Gran, let me start at the beginning. You see, this is my Serene Miss Smith I've been writing to you about."

Mrs. Durbridge didn't look like a woman given to boggling, but she really did boggle. I didn't blame her.

She started again : "William—" then as something registered, "William, am I mad, or is that Wilhelmina?"

Mr. William said : "Yes, and Serena and I are taking her up to her mother in Christchurch on the two-thirty flight from Momona. Gran, I don't know how you got here like this, but for goodness' sake hear me out. We've not got much time. Bunty will fill in the blanks after we leave, no doubt. And as she thinks Serena a combination of all the virtues, she may satisfy you.

"In brief, Miss Smith *is* my secretary. Jeff got badly injured down at the Pole. No, it's all right, he's on the mend. Kitty flew into my office last week. She'd been coming to spend the New Zealand winter with Jeff in

Christchurch anyway . . . and she dumped Wilhelmina on me. I was completely stumped because Bunty had been thrown off her horse and was just hobbling round.

"Miss Smith is a minister's daughter" (I had to hide a grin because it was evident Mr. William was trying to make it sound as respectable as possible) "and so, of course, accustomed to helping out in emergencies in her father's parish, and was sporting enough to come out here to help. You've no idea what Wilhelmina is like—she needs a bodyguard every moment—and I've not been here. I only got back at ten this morning— I've been up with Kitty.

"I flew back to pick up Wilhelmina and Serena to fly up with them today. I couldn't manage my niece on my own on the plane. I've got Kitty a motel—Jeff's mother is with her—and Serena and I will fly back tomorrow and try to pick up the threads of the business on Monday."

He stopped, blinked, and assumed an expression that said he knew there was something else he had to explain.

His brow cleared. "And she dyed her hair mouse because she was sick to death of looking glamorous. It cost her two jobs. Once a wife was jealous. Another time her boss's mother got suspicious of her. She was determined to sing small when she came to me. However, that didn't stop me falling for her," (I turned scarlet) "but she was so brassed off with employers and she kept me at arms' length, let me tell you —till now, when she's only softened up because of Wilhelmina !"

He paused for breath and his astute grandmamma got right to the crux of the matter. "Then where does this Veronica come into the picture?"

Well, I wanted to hear the answer to that one myself.

Mr. William made an impatient gesture. "She doesn't come into any picture now."

His grandmother said : "Just the same, I want to know about it . . . right pronto."

At that moment Wilhelmina began jumping up and

down, clinging to my hand, and it caught Mr. William's attention.

He said : "Serena, I'm afraid that brat wants the powder-room again. You'd better scram with her."

I knew he was grateful to his small niece. He'd rather explain Veronica to his grandmamma when I was not about. I hurried Wilhelmina to the house, calling out to Hayley and Bunty as I fled past them that Mrs. Durbridge had arrived.

By the time Mr. William and his grandmother reached the house (so the explanations must have been lengthy) I had showered and popped Wilhelmina in and out of a bath, giving her no time to play, and felt better able to face the matriarch.

Wilhelmina looked positively angelic in the cutest little blue suit, white socks, blue shoes, and I'd drawn her curls back into a ponytail. I'd donned my travel suit, thankful it was so subdued—brown and cream. I brushed my hair till it shone (as far as mouse *could* shine) and went very lightly on the make-up.

No one could have been more prim and proper than I, at the lunch-table, taking very little part in the conversation, as befitted an employee suddenly thrust into the bosom of the family. Mr. William tried to draw me out, but I wasn't having any. I enveloped Wilhelmina in one of her sensible pinnies and devoted myself to seeing she ate up her dinner.

Mrs. Durbridge unbent a little, but only as far as politeness demanded. She and Bunty talked as old friends, however, and I was grateful to Bunty for the few words of appreciation she said about me to this formidable atom.

Suddenly Mr. William said, narrowing his eyes, "Well, your months in the States have certainly rejuvenated you, Granny. You look ten years younger."

I told myself I must have just imagined I saw a blush creep up that well-preserved cheek.

But really there was hardly any time to sort out impressions. Mrs. Durbridge was surprisingly sweet with the child. Apparently she had seen her some months ago when she had first gone to the States, but most of the time they had been hundreds of miles apart. You could see the grandmother had a strong sense of family.

Underneath it all I was conscious of deep dismay. If only Mrs. Durbridge had come a week later, a month. Not now, not now, my heart cried to my mind.

And how different would it be at the office from now on? It was a bad start. Certainly, Mr. William had reacted splendidly. He hadn't let me down at all, or seemed even embarrassed—but how much did he have to dance to his grandmother's piping?

Only time would show.

At the airport I couldn't help a thrill of pride at being escorted by Mr. William and knew a little natural mischief at the glances directed at us as we stood awaiting our call, looking exactly like a family unit.

Mr. William twinkled urbanely. "They can't make out which of us she resembles most, we're so obviously her parents!

It was a superb day for flying. Soaring up from Momona you saw great hills carved out by time into a peninsula that cradled the harbour, and to the west lay range upon range of hills that in other countries would have been called mountains.

The spine of the Southern Alps came into view, seeming limitless, reaching towards the West Coast, a narrow province skirted on the far side by the Tasman Sea, great silver rivers threading down from the gorges and rushing towards the ocean. The farmsteads looked so far between, and lovely in their loneliness.

We went straight to the hospital from Harewood, the International Airport, in a taxi. It was fairly late in the afternoon by now. Jeff was still in a single room, lying very flat and heavily bandaged about the head, but his eyes lit up at the sight of his daughter, whose natural exuberance had to be curbed when she kissed her daddy.

I kept in the background as much as possible, but they wouldn't allow me to. They drew me in, Mrs. Ralston, Kitty, Jeff, Mr. William, but presently, because Wilhelmina couldn't be expected to remain still for too long, I suggested I'd take her outside by the Avon and watch the ducks and the boats.

They joined me there and we got a taxi and went out to the motel. Mrs. Ralston was quite charming. I thought wistfully that it would have been nice had Mrs. Durbridge been like her. She was so easy to get to know. Perhaps the knowledge that I'd looked after her little granddaughter while her son was seriously ill helped. Also, in our church up north we'd had an American family for a year on exchange, and they actually came from the same mid-western town as Mrs. Ralston and they had told me so much about it, I was able to talk about it with a basic familiarity.

Mr. William and Kitty went off to the hospital again at night. Mrs. Ralston and I put Wilhelmina to bed in the room I would share with her and we made a bed up for Mr. William on the divan in the living-room. He and I didn't have a moment alone.

To these folk, of course, I was nothing but Mr. William's secretary, brought into the family in an emergency. If Kitty suspected any more tender bond she hid it well, for which I was most glad. It would have been embarrassing otherwise with nothing declared between us. Yet I was still sure.

There was still the ride back together in the plane to look forward to. This time there would be no boisterous two-year-old to keep amused. I had a feeling Mr. William would feel it his duty to go straight out to Tattoo Bluff to see his grandmother after so long away ... and so unorthodox a homecoming ... but enough could be said in the semi-privacy of a double plane seat to keep me happy, I was sure.

At supper-time, when Kitty and Mr. William had returned from hospital, relaxed because Jeff seemed to be improving every hour, Mr. William suddenly said: "I called round at N.A.C. to find out what they'd managed to get us for tomorrow, Serena, and what do you think? We've got to go back separately. I'm on the late one. You can take a taxi from the airport and I'll go straight out to Tattoo Bluff. Isn't it annoying?"

Annoying? The understatement of the year as far as I was concerned!

I comforted myself with the thought that Mr. William would undoubtedly come with me in the taxi out to Harewood. I felt breathless and tired and frustrated at all that had happened and the way it had happened. But there was bound to be an oasis of sharing sandwiched in somewhere in this desert of being separated, surely.

But what happened? Mrs. Ralston came with us to the airport . . . just for the ride!

Kitty proposed it, Mrs. Ralston accepted joyfully, Mr. William and I could do nothing but say with commendable, if insincere enthusiasm, "Of course . . . why don't you?"

I caught Mr. William's eye and for one horrible moment thought we were both going to laugh aloud. I felt quite weak with relief when the danger was over. I'd blotted my copybook enough in his family circle. His formidable grandmamma was a cloud on my bright horizon.

Yet that interlocking of glances, the knowledge that we didn't need words, restored my confidence.

I was surprised, as we stood by the barrier, chatting inconsequentially, as one does at these times, at how much I hated that silver-winged monster squatting on the tarmac, because it was going to bear me away from Mr. William till Monday morning. And on Monday morning Grandmamma would descend upon Durbridge's. Would I become her secretary now? Would I never again be alone in an office with Mr. William?

Our call came—I mean my call. I shook hands with Mrs. Ralston. I wanted to shake hands, as any secretary might, with Mr. William, last of all. I'd taken off my glove so I could carry into the plane with me the warmth of his clasp.

"Goodbye till tomorrow, Serena," said Mr. William, oh, so casually, and leaned forward and kissed me full on the lips.

It was very fleeting. I turned hastily and positively dived through the opening, but as I went I heard Mr. William behind me say most urbanely to Mrs. Ralston, "We Durbridges always kiss our secretaries goodbye ... it's an old family custom."

I turned at the top of the gangway and waved. They waved back. I watched them, framed in the oval of the window, till we were off across the runway. I sat in a dream all the way, thankful for a companion who was an elderly man, who put his head on his chest the moment we were up and went straight off to sleep. I couldn't bear small talk to overlay that moment, I needed to savour it to the full right away.

Not even the thought of facing a business week with Mrs. Durbridge disturbed my dreams that night.

At lunch on that eventful Saturday morning, Mr. William had said, "Better have Monday morning off, Serena. This has certainly been no forty-hour week for you. You must be worn out."

His grandmother had said, surveying me like an exhibit at a show, "Your Serene Miss Smith looks capable of tackling anything, William. I don't think she needs—or would welcome—our concessions."

But he had said to me, on the way to the airport, "But I'll be downright annoyed if you set foot in the office one minute before morning-tea time. That's an order."

It was an order that wasn't going to be obeyed. Mrs. Durbridge was going to see that I was not trading on the fact that I had helped the family in a spot of bother.

It was not to be expected, of course, that Mrs. Durbridge would come in later than Mr. William, for she'd need to come in with him in the car, but if, as Mr. William vowed, he was *not* under her thumb, then no doubt at lunch-time he'd make the opportunity to take me out. And this time I'd not say no. His days belonged to the firm. But his time off I thought—and hoped—would be his own.

It seemed strange that the shop should look much

as usual. The odd-job man, a pleasant old chap, cleaning the windows, the usual bunch of girls in the cloakroom chatting. Word must not have reached them yet that the Old Girl was back. I said nothing.

I slipped along to my office at three minutes to nine, heart beating fast. Mrs. Durbridge might even think I should be in the outer office now. I had an idea that my office might have been Mr. William's and the sanctum that was now his, Mrs. Durbridge's, before her visit to the States.

I must be prepared for changes. She was going to be just like Maude Reedway, sure everyone liked Lance solely for his money. I'd have given a lot to know how Mr. William had explained Veronica Boleyn away. I had a hard, tight little knot in my middle at the very thought.

The door into Mr. William's sanctum was closed and I could hear his voice. Talking to his grandmother, no doubt.

I sat down, put my bag into a drawer, picked up some papers. It was hard to know where one had left off ten days ago. But I wanted to look busy, efficient, impersonal, when the dragon should emerge from her lair. Everything I'd *not* seemed when Mrs. Durbridge had first laid eyes upon me!

But she wasn't there. He was obviously speaking on the phone. His office was divided from mine by a partition that did not reach right to the ceiling and telephone conversations were audible in both.

I don't know what he'd been saying first, but what he said next impinged on my ears. Not only on my ears but on my heart, that foolish, trusting, vulnerable heart of mine.

He said: "Molly!" in really shocked exclamation. "How absurd can you get, goose? Only the girl next door! Now look, I'm not going to let you get an inferiority complex over this. You took the Veronica episode far too seriously. What was she but a flash-in-the-pan? An infatuation! Nothing more. All chaps have them, I suppose. No, you chump, it's not likely at all to recur after marriage. Anyway, that's up to you.

You can't hold it against a man for ever. It didn't mean a thing. *She's* not that sort of girl a chap wants to *marry*. Just you remember that. But you *are*. Now look, Molly, I'll—"

But I'd heard enough. I couldn't face him. Especially when his grandmother might come in any moment, not needing the formality of a knock. This wasn't the time or the place to have it out with him. Have what out with him? For after all, what had he said to me? Exchanged no vows, made no promises.

So on that last word overheard, I slid my chair back silently and tiptoed out of the office. I went into the buying-room, began sorting out some samples, what for goodness only knows. It was just something to occupy my hands, to provide an excuse to the rest of the staff, for not being in my own office.

My pulses were throbbing sickeningly . . . not for the reason they had throbbed during the weekend, but with pure, unadulterated rage. I was glad of that rage, it stopped me from feeling that deeper hurt, right in the core of my being.

Infatuation, he had said, speaking of his feeling for Veronica. Well, that was all this was going to mean in *my* life . . . nothing but infatuation. For a man who wasn't worth a tuppenny damn. He was exactly like I had at first summed him up . . . a lightweight, a trifler.

I wondered if Molly would hear about me. Though what was there to hear? His grandmother wouldn't be likely to tell about that kiss in the hay. She might approve of Molly . . . his girl-next-door. The girl who was the sort men married. Not just amused themselves with. I writhed. I felt so humiliated.

That was the worst of these charmers. They knew so well how to enchant a woman . . . quoting poetry, giving meaning glances, being audacious. And women fell for it . . . hook, line and sinker, as he himself had once remarked on the phone. Something struck me . . . he'd been talking to Molly that time. How odd. But what did it matter? It had sounded cheap, anyway.

The plainer men, the inarticulate ones, weren't

appreciated half enough. The ones who were so prac-
tised in casting a spell weren't the marrying sort.
Though—my thoughts halted in their indignant con-
demnation—apparently he *was* meaning marriage ...
with Molly, who sounded nice. Too nice for William
Durbridge!

Molly, who'd been horribly disturbed about Veronica
Boleyn ... and no wonder. I thought of the flowers Mr.
William had sent Veronica, the stole, the nylons.
Apparently she'd got wind of it. Well, who wouldn't?
I knew about the flowers, of course. He'd made me
order them ... to pay me out for turning him down
at first, I supposed. But apart from that I'd seen him
out with her several times. In a city of a hundred
thousand people, you couldn't keep things like that
secret.

Had they quarrelled over it? And had he made up to
me out of pique, or because he had the habit? And it
meant that that kiss we had shared and which he had
pretended meant something to him too had meant
nothing permanent.

I bit my lip till it bled, turning over swatches for
pyjama material and jotting down serial numbers that
weren't needed and which my pencil was registering
quite automatically.

I was trying to decide what to do. Would I go in
and if he said I ought to have taken longer off, say:
"Oh, I was here at nine, but you were having a private
conversation so I left you to it," and look at him
meaningly and with contempt?

But could I manage that at this moment, feeling as
I did? I was too afraid I'd only look wounded, disillusioned, which would only feed his vanity? Or I
might burst into tears.

But have patience, Serena ... the longer you hang on
to your temper the better it will be. He won't think so
much of himself by the time I've finished with him!
Oh, dear, just as well Father doesn't know what vin-
dictive thoughts his darling little Serena is cherishing
at the moment. I pushed that thought aside. Being a
daughter of the manse had its drawbacks. I told myself

it would be good to show this man that one female, at least, was not taken in by him.

To appear to have lost interest in him would wound him far more than flashing eyes and denunciation. My mind was made up. The longer I could postpone the final spurning, the less likely he was to realise that I could have heard that conversation and be acting from chagrin.

Molly could have him! I didn't envy her the life she'd have, never sure of him. If a man couldn't be constant now, when he was intending to marry Molly, what would he be like as a husband? At the thought of him marrying Molly I was furious to find my bottom lip trembling.

I pulled myself together.

It was half an hour later that Mr. William came into the buying-room.

"Oh, Serena! Glad you took my advice and had an extra hour in bed this morning. Better nip along and have a cup of tea. I've had mine."

I managed to say quite calmly, "Oh, having had breakfast later than usual I don't need one. May I finish this?" (Hoping he wouldn't ask what.) "Or do you need me right away?"

"In about ten minutes, Serena."

I said, not meeting his eyes, but keeping them on my notepaper, "Better be back to Miss Smith, Mr. William."

He chuckled, squeezed my elbow lightly and said: "Yes . . . for business hours only."

I found I was gritting my teeth.

He said, "Gran was tired out this morning; the old warhorse doesn't usually admit it. So she's not coming in till tomorrow. She and I are going to have a long talk over business affairs tonight."

Good! That meant he couldn't ask me out and it would give me time to adjust my mind and emotions to this, and when he did ask me, I could sound deflatingly casual about turning him down. I was going to enjoy that refusal.

Though at the moment all I felt was desolate.

I got through the day.

I felt I accomplished this only by being terrifically busy. Naturally with us both away for a week, work had piled up and we both worked at speed.

He said with a grin, "I want things fairly up to date for Gran tomorrow."

I said thinly, "I imagine so. I'd not like to cross her. Or fail her ... if I were you, I mean, of course."

"Oh, not to worry, my dear Miss Smith. I put Gran completely in the picture last night as far as you were concerned. Told her exactly what you were like ... how you had treated me at first and how you had just thawed. I also told her why."

I was startled and looked up, meeting his eyes fully for the first time that day.

"Told her why? You mean—"

"I told her you had had trouble with employers. Well, I mentioned that when first you met her—" he laughed reminiscently—"but I enlarged on it. Told her about your first boss's wife and your second boss's mother. I also told her Lance Reedway had actually taken up studies and was now a candidate for the ministry all because of you."

I said hastily: "Mr. William, that's just not right. I'm sure he didn't do it to—to win me over—to stir my interest. If he did he wouldn't be worth his salt and—"

His voice was very patient. "Serena, believe me I didn't mean to belittle in any way what he's done. I merely meant that because of you he'd begun thinking that way. I feel your words really jolted him. He'd had a pretty easy life, with a good business dropped into his lap, and he'd been content to drift. Now, don't tell me that's what I did. I've never found drapery easy. In actual fact, I detest it." I was amazed to see his hand tighten and whiten on his ball-point.

"I'm not sneering at Lance. It was he who said it about his future calling. I think you inspired him. I believe he's most sincere about it. I think he'll make a good minister ... perhaps all the better since he's had a considerable experience of life before entering it." He stopped, chuckled, said : "I'm amazed at myself. I'm practically selling him to you. I must be mad—it's the last thing I'd want to do. You have a terrific effect on us all, Serena. Make us more candid than is comfortable."

Candid . . . a man who was playing about with no less than three girls !

How grateful I was that at that moment the head of the underwear department rushed in, full of indignation.

"Mr. William !" she exclaimed. "This is simply ridiculous. The window-dresser is taking out my centre display and giving it to the hosiery department ! I put a lot of thought into the emphasis of that window—on certain lines—and I've had a sales analysis made and we're up on those goods compared with last month when I was in one of the back windows. I just won't stand for it. I can't run a department like this."

Mr. William got up, patted her shoulder. "Now, Miss Dempsey, we'll go into it. Has Mr. McGillivray started having the stuff taken out? No? Well, we'll go down immediately and see him. Of course, I'll have to have Miss Hadwell's ideas too. Perhaps *she* feels *her* displays aren't prominent enough. By the way, I did admire that display you've put up under the centre skylight in your department. And the wording of the tickets is particularly well done."

I decided I wouldn't have his job for anything. Sorting out petty differences like this must be hard on a man who'd rather be dipping sheep or sowing winter wheat. I caught myself up on that softening thought immediately. If I was going to mellow towards him every hour or so then I must have it bad. Watch it, Serena . . . if you find the going too hard you'd better look for another job. He'll be right . . . look at the masterly way he handled that. A couple of more compliments on the way down and Fighting Dempsey, as she was known throughout the shop, would be eating out of his hand. He knows women.

When I said goodnight to him at five-thirty he said, locking a drawer, "Goodnight, Serena . . . it's all right, girl, no need for 'Miss Smith' when we're quite alone. You've been awfully quiet all day ... was the weekend too much for you?"

"That was it," I said, not too readily to be suspiciously eager for an excuse. "I think I'll have a few early nights this week."

He nodded slowly. "Yes. I expect to be tied up with Granny, anyway."

Evidently confident that I would go out with him when he wasn't! I held my anger in check. It would be much more effective, later, to turn down a direct invitation.

He said, harking back to our previous conversation with a suddenness that disconcerted me, "I also told my grandmother that most girls would have been swept off their feet by that gesture of Lance Reedway's, but not you. That you weren't encouraging him at all. Which is very wise, seeing it wouldn't get him anywhere."

The effrontery of that enraged me. I managed to say quietly : "Nothing has been quite as definite as that, Mr. William. You seem to have read more into my attitude towards Lance than exists. He's been up home a lot, you know." I paused and couldn't help adding : "He's a different man from what he used to be. His studies last year have certainly widened his horizons. I find I've more in common with him than I used to have. Well, goodnight again, Mr. William," and I got myself out of the office.

Much later that night Father said to me : "Serena, what on earth is the matter with you? You're prowling about like a discontented tigress. How very unlike you."

Mother said, quite sharply, "Leave her alone, Angus. It's good for Serena not to be so placid. She's not been like her old self for months. And now she is. Serena, why don't you go out for a good walk?"

Her face was quite bland. I suddenly realised Mother knew I was in love. (That I *had* been in love. Because I wasn't now, my eyes had been opened.) Oh, horrors .. *and she favoured Mr. William.* She'd never wanted her daughters to marry into manse life, and she was a wee bit nervous about Lance Reedway.

With the promptitude of a stage cue the phone rang. I answered it.

Lance! I could have giggled.

"Do you want Father, Lance?"

"No, I don't, Serena. You know perfectly well I don't. You were tied up with that wretched boss of yours all last week—you can spare *me* a little time this week."

"Oh, can I?" I said, laughing a little. I wanted time to think.

"Yes. Some of the students are getting a party to see that play at the Majestic. We can get a big block of seats together. How about coming with me? It's Wednesday night."

Wednesday night. Mr. William had said he wanted a night or two with his grandmother . . . he might ask me later in the week. Nice if I had a genuine date and could make that the reason for my refusal.

So I said: "Oh, I'd love to come, Lance. Would you like to come up for dinner that night?"

Out of the corner of my eye I saw Mother's knitting needles pause, then get clicking again. I knew she wasn't pleased by the deep breath she released.

Then as Lance agreed I said, "All right . . . would you like to pick me up at the back door of the shop, in Great King Street?"

(There were two staff doors, the more convenient one led on to George Street, but the Great King one was where Mr. William parked his car.)

I hung up and settled down, spurning Mother's suggestion of walking, and lost myself in my book, all to give her the idea that now Lance had rung me I was more content. I did not dare risk Mother encouraging Mr. William. It would be too humiliating. Mr. William was going to find that one girl, at least, had lost interest in him.

Things worked out quite well for me. I managed to maintain a not too marked air of indifference. I didn't want to be too dramatic in my rejection ... at first.

Tuesday was so busy for Mr. William that he was hardly in the office. I had stacks of work to catch up on and was determined his grandmother should find nothing to cavil at. If she thought there had been too much personal association between us, at least she wasn't going to be able to say that because of it there had been slackness.

Mr. William did say: "Now, Miss Smith, you're working as if all the hounds of hell are on your heels. You don't need to catch up all in two days, you know, though I was glad Gran took today off too."

I shrugged. "I hate not having things up to date. It makes me feel untidy in my mind."

He chuckled. "Ah, yes. The Serene Miss Smith complex. The way you've disciplined your natural flair for unorthodox behaviour. But you ought not to do it. You'll probably develop all sorts of horrible inhibitions."

I looked at him over my typewriter. "But I find it works. That it makes life much easier. It had to slip a bit, naturally, when I got involved in your affairs because of Wilhelmina, but I'm glad to get back to steady routine now."

"What utter nonsense ... and I've no intention of allowing it. I like you much better as you were at Tattoo Bluff, Serena. I did find your former cold efficiency irritating, you know."

I grimaced. "I doubt that. It would irritate you far more to find my work full of mistakes. Mr. William, when your grandmother resumes work in the office, will we need to reorganise it? I mean I thought she might want your office and you mine. I could move into the outer office."

He stared. "My dear Miss Smith, Gran's been nothing more than a figurehead for the last two or three years. I know she looks young, but she *is* sixty-nine."

"I didn't think she could possibly be less. After all, you aren't exactly a boy, are you?"

He grinned. "I'm twenty-nine, if you're interested.

Just six years older than you. Gran was a mother at nineteen and my father a parent at twenty-one."

I said stiffly, not wanting to be involved in any personal discussion, "Yes, yes, I realised they must have been married young. But in any case, your grandmother is so ... so acute and alert I thought she would still hold the reins in her hands."

"Only nominally. She turned her office over to me some time back. Her big desk is still there. You can serve both of us."

My heart sank. It never worked.

He answered the phone. "Oh ... yes, all right, I'll see him in the buying-room."

He paused with his hand on the door handle, looked back over his shoulder and said : "And she isn't allowed to interfere in my private affairs, if that's what's worrying you, Miss Smith," and he was gone before I could retort that I was not.

Mrs. Durbridge was in the office when I arrived Wednesday. She was completely impersonal in her manner. We might never have met till now.

"Just carry on with your work, Miss Smith, as if I were not here, but see to it that Mr. William and I are not interrupted more than is necessary. Not, of course, that we wish to be inaccessible, if absolutely needed. I'll leave you to be judge of that."

It sounded to me as if she did indeed rule the roost. Over her shoulder Mr. William winked at me. I pretended not to see it.

Well, at least Mrs. Durbridge kept him busy and there was no time for other than business exchanges. I told myself that was simply splendid and what I desired above all things ... and went on feeling deadly flat.

At four Mrs. Durbridge was delighted to receive a call from an old acquaintance and went off with him to the cafeteria for some coffee.

Mr. William came into my office, looked over my typewriter, one hand each side of it, from the back of my desk. "Well, the dear dragon has departed, so I can get down to tintacks. Serena, I'm tied up tonight with Gran—heaven help me, she wants to go over the analysis of the Wednesday and the Friday sales for the last six months—but tomorrow night is gloriously free. I thought I'd never get you to myself again.

"She's going to see friends at Waitati. How about us going to see that play at the Majestic? I believe it's first-class."

I said calmly, with no sign of how my heart was heaving, "Sorry, Mr. William, but I'm going with Lance. Tonight. A whole bunch of divinity students and their girl-friends."

There was just a fraction of a pause before he said just as blandly, "Then how about a film tomorrow night? Or would you like a moonlight drive round the Peninsula?"

For one moment the utter felicity the latter would be flashed before me . . . cars with tiger-bright eyes purring round the shore road at the foot of the over-harbour hills . . . the countless tiny bays, the beacon light on Taiaroa Head, the moon rising over Harbour Cone . . . turning into the hills where pockets of bush still lingered, looking down on inlets and lagoons, and the leagues of ocean stretching to the South Pole.

Talking or not talking . . . finding a place to stop to watch the moon . . . a golden path on velvet waters . . . the lights of Dunedin on her seven hills . . . I clamped down on it, managed to say without too long a hesitation, "I'm afraid I'm booked tomorrow night as well, Mr. William. Lance must have been told about that moon too."

Mr. William's mouth set itself more squarely than ever. His chin was a shade more pugnacious. The light brown eyes looked deeply, suspiciously, into mine. But he suddenly relaxed and said, "Too bad. Well, some other time."

Conversations like this, in business hours, were most frustrating. You could never finish one satisfactorily. Phones rang, buzzers went, office staff popped in and out.

I felt an immense chagrin that he said nothing more.

He gave such strict attention to business when he came back from the buying-room that I felt it had hardly registered. It certainly hadn't put him off his stride.

But when we left the office together at five-thirty I could feel his eyes on me. I'd dressed very carefully that morning—black, which suited me even with my hair this uninspiring colour, and a burnt gold blouse that showed to perfection under the jerkin jacket. And I'd borrowed Mother's tourmaline necklace and Patsy's crocodile handbag that matched my shoes.

He looked a little surprised as I moved with him to the back door. "Don't you usually use the other door, Miss Smith?" (Some of the staff were with us.)

I said easily, "Yes, but I thought this would give Lance easier parking at this time of night. Father invited him up for tea. They have a lot in common, of course."

Mr. William glanced sideways at me. "I imagine your father gets on to terms with most people, Serena." (Staff had gone.)

"Yes, he's very much a man's man, but naturally there's something more about divinity students."

We picked our way across the rubble. There had been alterations and extensions to the furnishing department at the back of the shop and a lot of debris left lying.

"I hope this will be repaved by next weekend," said Mr. William. "I'm picking Gran up round the front. A bit rough for her—Oh, hullo, Reedway. Believe you're off to the play tonight. They tell me it's mighty amusing."

"Yes, practically all the Divs are going. We're putting on a play ourselves in aid of a new building for youth work in one of the new housing areas and thought it might give us a few wrinkles. We were told the stage effects are excellent but simple and ours leave a lot to be desired. We're giving our play a two-hour run-through tomorrow night under the eye of a chap who is supposed to be quite a critic."

I turned scarlet.

Mr. William answered Lance and began admiring,

in the way of all men, Lance's Peugeot. Then he said briskly to Lance, who must have thought it slightly odd, "Well, get in, Reedway, I'll see Serena into the other side."

He put a hand under my elbow and urged me round the back of the car where he said in a low voice tinged with contempt, "I detest liars, Miss Smith. And just what game *are* you playing? Trying to set one man off against another? Very despicable." His mouth gave a wry twist and he added : "In my case it was quite unnecessary, anyway."

By the time he'd finished uttering he had the door open, had handed me in, said "Goodnight, Miss Smith," and was gone.

CHAPTER EIGHT

I SEETHED with anger all the way up the hill and was immensely grateful to Lance for the small talk that enabled me to regain my composure.

Playing one man off against another! What colossal vanity! I should love to tell him so. Just because two other girls were apparently vying for his favours it didn't mean this one was! The nerve of it . . . to imagine I wanted to spur him on with the threat, the empty, false threat of competition!

Mr. William was extremely distant during the next few days, which made me madder than ever since I had intended to be the distant one. Oddly enough, though his grandmamma didn't exactly unbend, she didn't interfere much with me. And she was a trifle more absentminded than I'd imagined her. I'd thought of her as a gimlet-eyed, imperious autocrat, ready to pounce like a hawk on any small mistake.

She wandered round the shop and the vast reserves, no doubt making the assistants extremely nervous, but every now and then she'd stop and gaze into space. I saw her several times as I trotted round after Mr. William taking notes as needed. I liked that part of the work, it brought me into touch with the saleswomen and men. They were a grand bunch of workmates. That was why I liked being in a drapery office, it wasn't just facts and figures and letters.

I said this, about the staff, to Mr. Jennings. He nodded. "It's a very harmonious store to work in, thanks to Mr. William. He even toned his grandmother down. She was such a firebrand. Not that Mr. William is not a disciplinarian, but he's a very just one. But he's been frightfully tetchy the last few days. Has anything upset him, do you know? Or it could be that he's had control of the business so long that his grandmother's sudden return has put him on edge. He needn't worry, she's very thrilled with his administration."

I saw evidence of Mr. William's tetchiness later that day. This was the day of the month that the branch managers and some of their heads came to Dunedin. We had small branches in Oamaru, Milton, Balclutha, Gore. The manageress of the Gore Branch was up today.

After they had gone Mr. William called Mrs. Jennings into his office. They didn't ask me to move to the outer office so it was nothing private.

Mr. William sounded most irate. He snorted. "That woman! For some time I've been wondering why the Gore returns—on the women's side—haven't kept pace with the returns from the other branches. They're considerably down on the year before. Gore used to be one of the best. I've not been impatient because there are tides in these things. Some years certain districts can suffer financially because of local conditions. For instance, you remember, when South Otago had those disastrous floods. Some farmers were almost ruined. You'd expect a drop in the rag trade then. But there's been nothing like that.

"Today I suddenly tumbled to the reason. I looked at Mrs. Tundell. She was beautifully dressed, even exquisitely, so it wasn't a case of frumpishness affecting sales. In the world of fashion, as we know, you've got to keep up to the minute . . . in fact, beat the clock.

"But it hit me in the eye today. I tried her out. I said: 'Tell me, Mrs. Tundell, do you feel our buyers are keeping abreast of the times? Buying in the right styles, quantities, colours? Are we timing our deliveries right?' She agreed with everything. I didn't bawl her out, though I longed to. But I'll write her on the subject. I wanted to shout at her: 'Then why the devil did you buy your shoes, bag, gloves, blouse and suit all from some other firm than Durbridge's?' Confidence in our buyers . . . in our stock . . . Pah! For all I know even her stockings and underwear probably came from another firm!"

Mr. Jennings sounded just as indignant. He may have been just soothing Mr. William down by agreement, I wouldn't know, but the whole thing made me uneasy. I hoped I wouldn't be the next to have the mantle of Mr. William's displeasure fall upon me. In a business way, I meant. He already was displeased with me about pretending I was going out with Lance that night.

An hour later, near closing-time, Mr. William said to me, "You'd gather from what I said to Mr. Jennings that I think we've fathomed the exact reason for the dropping back in the Gore branch takings, Miss Smith?"

"Yes, Mr. William."

"Pretty poor, isn't it, when a woman lacks confidence in the very goods she's selling? I can't understand it. I didn't think there *were* better values than ours. It's something that always makes me mad . . . the girls buying elsewhere. I'll have to look into this Gore business. Must be something wrong. If a woman can pass her own stock, on which she'd get ten per cent house discount, to buy her clothes from our rivals, then she ought not to be working for us. I'll go down to Gore."

He paused, added: "That's something I've appreciated about you, Miss Smith. Apart from the clothing you had when you first came to us from Auckland, I've never seen you in goods other than Durbridge's."

I gulped, looked up at him and said unhappily,

because now the vials of his wrath would fall upon me, "Er—I—well, Mr. William, I just can't be a hypocrite and pass this off. I—er—I was passing Arthur Barnett's in my lunch-hour and fell for this winter suit. I just simply loved it, found it irresistible. I don't doubt we have lots of fascinating suits, but this was just me and I knew it. Look." I dived into a fixture behind me and brought out a parcel, slid my fingers under the transparent tape that secured the paper and opened it.

There it lay, my lovely new suit in vivid green with bands of soft, honey-coloured fur. I looked up, my expression rueful, I knew, and to my great relief Mr. William burst out laughing.

"Oh, Serena, you're so unpredictable, refreshingly candid where most girls would have been cagey. They would have told themselves that it was policy to keep mum. And yet for no reason at all the other night you—" He broke off, making a dismissing gesture with his hands. I could have finished it for him. He'd been going to say: "For no reason at all the other night, you lied to me."

So I found myself answering as if he'd finished it. He'd swung away from me, so I said to his back: "I had a very good reason, Mr. William, but I don't want to explain it."

He swung back, barked out, "Why?"

I couldn't hold his eyes.

He said, rather gently and sadly, but with something in his voice that hinted at strain, though I couldn't imagine why . . . surely a man who kept three girls on a string wasn't serious enough to feel strain about it? . . . "You know, Serena, I rather thought you were the tell-the-truth-and-shame-the-devil kind. As witness your dealings with your former employers. You didn't hesitate to tell Maude Reedway exactly what you thought even though you knew it would cost you your job. I thought you were too modern to be other than candid."

I said slowly, "I think it's easier, even in a modern world, for a man to be candid. We girls of this age are rather given to despising the subterfuges of the

Victorian world—as seen in novels—but in some ways it still isn't easy to be a woman."

Mr. William was staring at me. And of course at that moment when we were both cool and perhaps might have said exactly what was in our minds, Mr. Jennings came back.

Later that night I told myself it was just as well he had.

Dad had a meeting cancelled and Mother was out, so he said: "This is a gift from the gods, Serena, my love. Let's go to see that picture at the Regent."

I always enjoyed being out with Dad. We went to a lot of cricket and football matches together as a rule, but lately he'd had so many Saturday weddings we'd missed out.

Because we'd gone at the last moment we didn't get a very good seat. We managed to get upstairs, but not in the lower circle.

And right in the front centre seats ... Mr. William and Veronica Boleyn! So he wasn't even playing fair with Molly!

She was frightfully overdressed as always, I thought laughed too frequently and too shrilly. Honestly, the man must have no discrimination at all!

I hoped Father wouldn't notice Mr. William. Father just doesn't recognise delicate situations. Sometimes it has its uses. He'd never notice tension between two families in a parish, for instance, therefore they'd probably find themselves both invited to supper at the Manse and give in and be quite cordial to each other under his benevolent wing. And then they'd so get into the habit of it, their differences would melt like dew in sunlight.

If he saw Mr. William, it would be just like the Reverend Angus Smith to bowl up to him and say: "How about us all having coffee together?"

And I'd just as soon drink coffee with a—with a boa-constrictor as that creature. Veronica, I mean. I didn't mean to catch Mr. William's eye even. I didn't want him to think I was piqued about her when next I refused his suggestion of an outing. (If he ever asked me again!) I wanted him to realise I just couldn't be bothered with him, that I had no interest in him whatever.

I could hardly have told what the film was about. I tortured myself by gazing at the back of Mr. William's head. It was a very shapely head, with short cropped hair and a well-curved back. How good it would feel, returning a kiss, to put one's hand against that curve ... heavens, I was getting positively maudlin. I must be mad!

Dad was chuckling away beside me in his infectious way that always set everybody else laughing. He leaned towards me. "Serena, aren't you enjoying this?"

"Oh, I am, tremendously, Dad." But I'd quite lost the thread of the story and hoped he didn't recap too much when we got home.

When it was over, I propelled Father towards another exit. Out of the tail of my eye I saw Mr. William adjusting Veronica's shoulder cape and saw Veronica looking into his face and smiling. He returned the look with interest, patted her hand.

Well, who cared?

He put an arm about her shoulders to guide her out into the aisle. I saw him recognise another couple and realised they all knew each other. The other girl looked completely natural and lovely beside Veronica's brassiness. She had smooth, nut-brown hair, glossy and attractively dressed with never a sign of tinting, a wild-rose complexion, beautiful teeth. She had a handsome companion with her.

I suddenly felt drab and unsought. Just a girl out with her father. Which of course was perfectly ridiculous. Mr. William *had* asked me out and I had turned him down, the other week. There was no reason in the wide, wide world why he shouldn't ask another. By the time I did get to sleep that night I told myself I knew why I was taking this so badly, why I felt so disillusioned ... I wanted above all things to feel Mr. William was worthy of being loved. I hated to think that he played fast and loose with his Molly.

Not only that, but from that overheard telephone conversation, I knew perfectly well that he was serious about her, thought of her in terms of marriage, so it put *me* on a level with Veronica... just a good-time girl. Someone he was attracted to in a purely superficial kind of way, nice to accompany to certain things, to make love to in a light fashion... but Molly was for keeps. And he *had* promised Molly it was all over, just a flash-in-the-pan. He was a fool. Molly might have seen him tonight.

I turned my pillow over again, thumped it, said sternly to myself that it no longer mattered to me, any of it. No more hankering after him. *Your* fancy for *him* could have been just a flash-in-the-pan too, Serena Smith! He's attractive, yes, very, in fact dangerously so... that voice of his, that mouth, that irresistible chuckle... but that's all there is to him—charm!

Oddly enough I did then fall asleep, so I told myself the next morning that it proved it was all a matter of discipline and common sense. But I wouldn't use Lance any more. It wasn't fair.

I'd no sooner got settled at my desk, taking up where I'd left off last night, when Mr. William breezed in.

"Oh, good morning, Miss Smith. Look, have you got anything important on in your lunch hour?"

How wonderful. My opportunity!

I found an exquisite pleasure in saying: "No, I have not, Mr. William, but I'm not coming out to lunch with you today or any other time. I find this quite tiresome. So much so that if you insist on pestering me I shall have no other course than to find a position where I shall merely be an employee."

To my immediate chagrin he burst out laughing. And to deepen my humiliation his grandmamma came in, en route for the inner office.

He waited till she'd gone in... but I knew she was still in earshot... and he said, still shaking, "Oh, my Serene Miss Smith! How you do bite! I was *not* asking you out to lunch. I was trying to find out if you had any private appointments, because you're coming to

Gore with me. I hasten to add that Mr. Jennings is coming with us. In fact, so is Mrs. Jennings. She often does. She has relations in Gore and it gives her the chance to see them." He laughed again. "Ever hear of the famous 'Betty Baxter, who refused a man before he axed her?' Well, that's you!"

I'd never felt so humiliated in my life. If I wasn't fair I wouldn't blush so easily. I detest it. And at that moment Mrs. Durbridge came out of her office again and stood staring.

I looked across at her and decided on candour. "Mrs. Durbridge, in case you have any wrong ideas about— about Mr. William and me—and what you've just heard, I'm going to tell you that I have no personal interest in your grandson at all. I've just said to him that if we can't keep this relationship purely one of employer and employee I shall be forced to leave. I think he told you I've been put in awkward positions before. I'd rather get out now than face another upset."

To my complete amazement Mrs. Durbridge burst out laughing. It was the first time I'd ever seen any resemblance between her and Mr. William.

She said, gasping, "When I think of what William wrote me about his new secretary while I was in the States, I just can't believe it! Well, all I can say, Miss Smith, is that you know your own business best and that you'll be very good for him. *I* was the one who proposed that he should take you to Gore with him. I've always believed in our employees getting a full insight into our organisation. And William, stop pestering Miss Smith. If she doesn't want to go out with you, she doesn't have to. Don't make her uncomfortable. She's the best secretary we've ever had, we don't want to lose her. You ought to be glad she's this way. Some of your former secretaries have positively angled for your attentions. But it's quite all right today, Miss Smith, his invitation is purely business."

She made me feel much better . . . as if I hadn't made an idiot of myself . . . as if we had been dealing with nothing more than a troublesome small boy.

If only Mr. William had looked in the slightest abashed. But he just chuckled irrepressibly, gathered up some papers, said, "Right, Miss Smith, since you gave away the fact that you're absolutely free this dinner-hour, you can't escape going to Gore with us. You'd better ring your mother and tell her we'll be back fairly late tonight. It is, after all, ninety miles or more. No, stay, I'll ring her. Go and get your bonnet on. I want to get away."

I was perversely glad that I had on the green suit from Arthur Barnett's.

As he handed me into the big Chev I said: "It looks as if I'd have had time to have rung my mother myself since Mr. Jennings isn't here yet."

"Oh, when Gran proposed this at breakfast, I rang him and told him not to bother coming to the shop, that we'd pick him up at his place."

I said slowly: "We live on West Hill too... he's my father's session clerk. You could have saved me the trip down as well."

I was past caring about speaking tactfully to my boss. In fact he'd ceased to be that to me.

His voice was hatefully suave. "But, Miss Smith, surely you realise why. If I had you would undoubtedly have found you had a pressing appointment in town in your lunch-hour. Isn't it a glorious day? Autumn down south is really something. Always reminds me of Scotland in autumn. That's the idea, you know, visit England in spring, Scotland in autumn."

I said distantly, "I'm not really expecting to travel as far as that. I don't suppose I'll ever have the money."

"You never know. Depends who you marry. Drapers travel in the course of their business. Even impecunious Divinity students seem to manage it to further their studies. And in any case, my lass, Lance isn't an impecunious one. He has a wealthy mother behind him."

I took a tight rein on my temper.

When I didn't answer, he turned and surveyed me. "No wonder you fell for that colour, Serena. Only one thing could improve it... if your hair was blonde. You'd look dazzling then."

There was something I wanted to say and it reminded me. He might tell me to mind my own business, but—

"Mr. William, about Mrs. Tundell and her wearing nothing from Durbridge's that day. I expect it was, like my suit, just an odd purchase. I expect everything else she has comes from our shop. I mean our stuff can't be bettered for quality and price, it's just that occasionally one sees something in another shop and falls in love with it.

"I heard the girls in the cloakroom one day. One of the office girls said : 'Let me get my smock on quickly. I don't want Mr. William to see my frock. He'd know immediately it didn't come from downstairs.' I was rather surprised, Mr. William. I—we—you and I haven't always seen eye to eye on—on personal matters —but I have admired your fairness with your staff. Especially your policy that—that the customer isn't always right.

"But I don't like this particular attitude. It's very restricting to have to always shop in one store, and you're making the staff feel guilty if they make as much as one purchase outside. There, I've got that off my chest, and you can tell me it's nothing to do with me if you like—and you would be quite justified."

We were heading out through Caversham. He negotiated some traffic, then turned and looked at me briefly. There was nothing but pure friendliness in his eyes. "Serena, although there are times when I could cheerfully choke you—that's entirely a personal thing— at this moment I can only admire you. I detest pompous executives and have always prided myself on not being one, but on this matter—staff purchases—I seem to have been a bit one-eyed. Once you get the backs up other rebellions can follow. I do like my staff to come to me and point out a better policy, but naturally some are a little diffident about such things. But you've spoken out knowing you ran the risk of incurring my displeasure. If I act on your advice—let the staff know that while I expect them to purchase the bulk of their needs from us, I've no objection to the occasional purchase elsewhere—I'm sure it will make for a better relationship. Thank you."

A traitorous, foolish warmth flowed over me. So I said hastily, as we drew up in front of the Jennings' home, "Thank you, Mr. William, I appreciate that. Now, would you like Mr. Jennings in front with you? You may have business to discuss."

He shook his head. "No, it'll be nice for the Jennings to be together. They're a devoted couple, aren't they? And I think the four of us should just enjoy the drive and forget about business till we get there. When I'm driving I'm always more interested in what's in the paddocks than in drapery."

He got out and walked round the front of the car. He stepped on to the pavement, then came back to my window, which I had opened. He leaned his arms on the window-ledge, which brought his face quite close to mine, and his eyes on a level with my own.

"I'm particularly glad you had the courage to bring that subject up right now. I had been going to take it up with Mrs. Tundell when I arrived. How insufferably impertinent of me." He wrinkled his nose. "What a delightful perfume . . . reminds me of the East. What is it? Sandalwood, I bet."

I couldn't help laughing. "Right in one! And it, at least, is from Durbridge's cosmetic counter!"

I watched him go whistling up the path. This was a steep suburb and the Jennings' home was built on steps and terraces, bright with sun-plants and lit in all the corners with the glowing, jewel-rich colours of dahlias.

I'd not been farther south than Dunedin, so it enchanted me, this road. I'd been into Central Otago visiting the lakes and mountains, but we'd gone direct westward, through Middlemarch, instead of south then west, so it was all new country beyond the airport.

We stopped beside Lake Waihola for morning tea where we had home-made scones with strawberry jam and cream, served by a woman with a pleasant Northumbrian accent. She seemed to know Mr. William, he must often call here. I thought, despairingly, for I'd rather think him a monster, he really is so interested in people.

The atmosphere, due to our being with the Jennings, became more relaxed. I knew them so well. Dad said he couldn't have had a better session clerk. Strange how, on the surface, one could enjoy oneself, despite the fact that buried deep down was a core of pain, at being so deceived.

Something struck me. "Isn't Waihola a strange name ... it's not really Maori at all. There's no L in the Maori alphabet."

"Dead right," said Mr. William. "It ought to be Waihora. It's a corruption. *Wai* ... water, *hora* ... spreading. The waters do spread because the basin of the lake is shallow, fed by the Waipori River and by the watershed of the hills right round it. Not like some of our Alpine lakes, gouged out by glaciers in the Ice Age. Of course this lacks the glorious colouring of the Central Lakes. They are snow-fed. This is mostly pewter-coloured. But it has a beauty all of its own at sunset-time. The lake gets stained rose-coloured then."

"And what does Waipori mean?"

"Oh, dark water. More correctly Waipouri. The river does come through a very dark gorge. Though in autumn the evergreen native forest is lit with the gold of English trees in patches. To see the sun filtering through the pure gold of the birches is really something."

I liked him knowing things like that. Lance, despite his now broadening interests, seemed very limited. I pulled myself up on the thought, comparisons were odious. And a trip like this, undisturbed by the antagonism that so often flared between Mr. William and myself, was likely to lull my distrust of him. He *was* a likeable fellow, no doubt of that. But in his dealings with women, completely unreliable.

Into my mind flashed that poem Mother had kept in a scrapbook from long ago. It was by Norma Davis of Tasmania. Mother vowed it had kept her from accepting her first love and waiting till she met Father who was all she'd dreamed of. I've an excellent memory for poetry. But I didn't want—or need—that poem now. It began :

"You have such charm of manner, and you know
  the potent power of a word, a touch..."

and finished :

"Your clear eyes glow so steadfast and so true
    It seems sheer sacrilege to harbour fears;
  And yet, and yet, each time I think of you
    Some dark bell peals dire warning in my ears."

Mother had then trusted that instinct, heeded the warning bell, and later events had proved her right.

I'd heed that warning bell too.

Talk continued on Maori names and meanings. I said : "I always wonder that the meanings in English aren't given on our signposts beneath the Maori names. The meanings are usually so beautiful—or at any rate interesting—and it would be so good for the tourists. I feel where they might forget the Maori names because they're unfamiliar with them, they might remember the translations."

Mr. William's eyes lit up. "How odd you should say just that, Serena. I'm taking it up with the Automobile Association. We're just getting warmed up to the possibilities of our tourist trade. We're getting far more Canadian and American tourists, for instance. After all, we're so short a distance—in time—from America now. And I'm quite sure that while tourists might forget that a river was named Taieri, they might easily remember that it meant The-tide-on-the-eleventh-night-of-the-moon. And it could also give our children a better knowledge of Maori. They would absorb the knowledge gradually without knowing they were."

Why, oh, why did he have to be such a kindred spirit, in all save that one thing ... constancy ... which was so important to marriage?

On we went ... Warepa, the fortified house ... Waipahi, the flowing waters (that was where they had overflowed the night Mr. William was coming up from Invercargill), Wairuna, the stream where dock grows,

Pukerau, the place of many hills...all these things lent enchantment to the day.

Mr. William said as we swung over the Mataura River (reddish, eddying water, so named because the swamp water draining into the lake is impregnated with oxide of iron), "I'll give Meddiford a ring from this box and find out where he's booked us in for lunch."

Before I thought I said: "Oh, does he know we're coming?"

Mr. William looked at me with a frown. "I'm not on a spying trip, Serena. Imagine walking in unannounced. You could catch your staff out in the most embarrassing situations."

When he'd disappeared into the phone box Mr. Jennings said: "He's a good lad. Plenty of bosses would do just that, but not Bill Durbridge."

I wasn't present at all the interviews Mr. William had with his staff—only when he needed me to take things down. Every now and then he shunted me off. Once he said he'd not need me for an hour and to go and explore the town; the other times he told me to prowl round the shop and to get to know the staff.

"Meet as many junior members as you can, Miss Smith. It makes for personal interest for them. I get them all up to the main store at some time or other. Makes them feel part of it. You aren't shy, are you? As a minister's daughter you'll be used to mixing with people. Off you go."

They seemed a very nice crowd. It wasn't a very busy day at the shop and it gave me the chance of getting to know the staff. One part of my mind warned me not to identify myself too closely with Durbridge's, that I might find it wiser not to stay in their employment, the other part—not my mind but my heart— urged me to stay on.

There were too many things to admire about Mr. William. He'd muttered as we drew up outside the shop, "Look at that window, Mr. Jennings...ever see such a mess? Handbags bang in the middle of lingerie.

And a glorious day like this they're showing raincoats. Even if it were wet here yesterday they could have whisked them out and substituted seasonal stuff that must be got rid of. They could get full price for it now, whereas if it hangs fire, prices will have to be slashed at the sales. Raincoats should always be shown where they can be removed without disturbing the balance of the display."

I expected, therefore, to see signs of that window being taken apart, to hear strips being torn off someone. But by the time the shop day had ended it had been done most tactfully. Mr. William had the heads of the departments in the staff room and after a cup of tea had given what was a very well constructed lecture on timing in display. As far as I could find out he'd not even ordered the things to be done tomorrow.

I asked Mr. Jennings about it on the quiet. "No, he'll wait and see if they act on their own initiative . . . I'm pretty sure of that. I've seen him in action so often I could guarantee it. He'll probably ring the manager tomorrow night and ask how the heads and the window-dresser reacted to his suggestions."

It was building up an image of Mr. William in my mind . . . kindly, knowledgeable, a man who had disciplined himself to take the shop life he did not like and to make a splendid job of it. A man who did not take advantage of his undoubted power to make his employee's lives miserable, even when they deserved it.

In his business dealings with his rivals, with the travellers, and in Durbridge's reputation for holding genuine sales and for truth in advertising, he was known for integrity. Yet in his dealings with women he was a gay deceiver. Oh, well, most of us had a flaw somewhere.

Father had seen to it that I had been told about mine.

"You pride yourself on your tolerance, Serena, yet you aren't truly tolerant, you know."

I'd cried hotly, "Well, I can't stand these narrow, carping Christians who are such killjoys!"

Dad's eyes had crinkled at the corners. "Think that one out, my stormy petrel ... if you aren't tolerant of the intolerant, can you really call yourself tolerant at all?"

... So much good in the worst of us, so much bad in the best of us ... but was a woman ever wise to let her heart rule her head in the matter of a man who couldn't be true?

No. Mr. William was not for me.

On the return journey, after dinner at the manager's, it was not till we got right to Milton that I realised we were leaving the Jennings there for the night. How clever of Mr. William not to have mentioned it before we started off this morning. Yet I couldn't have turned the trip down. He *was* my employer.

I knew the Jennings had a son farming in the district. Evidently he was going to run his father up to the city in the morning. It was only thirty-six miles.

"I won't expect you in before ten, Malcolm," said Mr. William to Mr. Jennings.

Mr. Jennings said : "Oh, no, thanks, Mr. William, I'll be there on time."

Mr. William said to the son, "I'm sure you can find a means of delaying him. You could have a cow in trouble or something. Malcolm works far too hard, can't hold him back. Well, cheerio, everyone, we'll be on our way."

It was a perfect night with a crescent moon over the Maungatuas, and although the sunset had gone, the after-glow still lingered as we reached Lake Waihola, tinging the edges with pink.

Mr. William said : "It ought to be called the Lake of the Sunset. It's sheer beauty now, don't you think? It's a duck-shooter's paradise."

"Do you go shooting?"

"No, I'm a birdwatcher. I do it with cameras."

I had my eyes on the darker water, reflecting the first faint stars now. I said idly, "Isn't it still? See how those bulrush heads are silhouetted against the lake, darker still. I must tell Mother. She could bring Father out here to get some. She loves them for church decoration."

Mr. William said : "We could get some now. No time like the present. Besides, it's very lovely down on the lake-shore."

I instantly regretted saying it.

Access to the bulrushes wasn't easy. The path threaded between willows that grew close and forced us together. Mr. William took my arm and I grew so breathless I found it hard to keep my voice even.

We came out on to a little beach with smooth banks of lake sand faintly rippled by the wind and stippled over by the countless arrow-marks of the feet of the water-fowl. Mr. William stopped, took his pipe out of his pocket and lit it, the flare of the match lighting up his features momentarily with a warm tenderness. Which meant nothing, I told myself, turning away my eyes to look over the waters.

At the far side were lights of farmhouses that snuggled into the valleys, some that climbed the hills . . . happy little homes, I hoped, where dreams had come true.

Suddenly Mr. William said : "Know that poem by Joan Pomfret, Serena?

'Houses seem so happy towards the close of day,
Firelight-filled and lamplit, their worries put away.
Easy to imagine lovely things behind
Amber-tinted curtain and shadow-haunted blind.' "

I knew my voice sounded jerky, because I didn't want it to betray any warmth. "No, I didn't know it. Nice, isn't it?"

Nice. When I knew it was perfect. Uttered by the one man who mattered. I hardened my heart.

I said, "Let's get these bulrushes, I don't want to be too late."

He took out his pocket-knife and began sawing them off. I had to hold them in both hands, we got so big a bunch.

We came back along the little lakeside path, and

just before we stepped out of the tree shadows, Mr. William stopped, caught me by the elbows and swung me round to face him.

I stood there, my bag on my arm and the bunch of rushes stiffly in my hands, almost like a palisade between us.

He'd put his pipe in his pocket.

"Serena," he said, "what went wrong? It was most frustrating, I know. I had to go to Christchurch just after—well, I was away a week and when I did get back there was Gran. Even the air services fought against us being together. The disruptions! But for them I'd have been home for a night before Gran arrived. Then we couldn't even come home on the same plane. So too much happened between."

I said as calmly as I could, "Between what? I don't know what you mean, Mr. William."

He gave me a little shake. "You do, you know. You're just pretending. I mean too much happened between that kiss we shared and our next chance of . . . of taking up where we left off."

I feigned surprise. "Oh, *that*! Why, Mr. William, aren't you making rather a lot of what was only an overcharged moment? A sentimental one. I didn't take it seriously. You know . . . some enchanted evening and all that. You can't recapture these things . . . nothing but the mood of the moment."

His grip tightened. "Frankly, Serena, I just don't believe you."

I tried to say something scornful and failed to find the words.

He went on, struck by a sudden thought. "Serena, I know! I'm a fool, I ought to have thought of it before. It's Veronica who's sticking in your crop. Well, I can explain that. It so happened that—"

I struck in, "It's nothing to do with Veronica. She just doesn't matter tuppence to me. Why should she?" (That was true enough. It was Molly who mattered.) "Look, Mr. William, we'll have to get this straight. If you can't get it into your head that I'm just not attracted to you, I've no other option but to look for another position. And—apart from all this hoo-ha—I like my job. I like the atmosphere of the shop better than any I've worked in. I like the staff, the way you treat them. But I'm just not interested in you personally. It's abominably difficult for a girl to keep turning a man down when he asks her out. She feels churlish. Pleads other engagements, hoping he'll get the message.

"She feels most uncomfortable about it, but it's kinder than encouraging a man she has no romantic feeling for. You've forced me to be brutally candid, but I think it's the only thing, Mr. William, in the circumstances."

There was a painful silence. Mr. William's grip had lessened.

Then he said in such a strange voice : "Serena, I just don't believe this. I'm sure there's some misunderstanding. Something happened. What went wrong? Could you—*can* you—possibly explain away a moment such as we two shared as . . . just the enchantment of a moment?" I didn't know what emotion had him in its grip, male mortification . . . hurt pride, bewilderment, or what?

I managed to say, despite my dry throat, "Then all I can say is that it must have meant more to you than it did to me." Then I swallowed. It had been physically painful to even say the words.

His grip tightened till it hurt. He shook me again much more savagely. "There's only one way to prove it. Get those damned bulrushes out of my face!" He brought up one hand and absolutely shoved them to one side against my shoulder and drew me as hard against him as was possible with my hands clenched into a knot round the stalks and keeping us a little apart.

His mouth found mine and with every bit of self-control and strength of mind I could summon up I fought the desire to respond to him.

And succeeded.

But if it had lasted ten seconds longer I'd have been undone.

As he took his lips from mine I said in a level tone

I was quite proud of, "These bulrush heads are marking my new suit!"

He let me go so abruptly I nearly fell.

He took the few strides to the water's edge, stood looking out over the waters from which every vestige of colour had now faded, and took out his pipe, relighting it.

He walked back, said, with a touch of wry humour, "Well, that's that. You couldn't have been more convincing. My apologies. I'll just have to take it."

I even schooled my mind and said to myself, "It's got him in his vanity. Serena, I'm proud of you."

He was punctilious about handing me into the car, but he didn't speak till we were away past Henley, threading round the Taieri River.

Then he said in a perfectly ordinary tone, "Well, you can stop worrying now, Serena. I won't pester you again. It's too tough on a girl, having to keep turning down her employer. Sorry I was so blind."

I could have wept. He would never know what it meant to me to reply, "Oh, thank you, Mr. William, that puts my mind at rest. I've not worked with all these months without knowing that you don't hold grudges. I've noticed that with the staff. Let's get back on to a normal footing. I did find it interesting at the Gore branch today. They're a particularly nice group of workers, I'd say."

"True. The manager is a grand chap. I had a talk with him about the mantle showroom, and asked why it had fallen behind. I wish he'd told me earlier, but I can understand he didn't want to gossip. Mrs. Tundell's husband walked out on her some months ago and it affected her work. One's personal life often does. She lost interest.

"Well, it seems it had all been a misunderstanding, due to some real malice on the part of another woman. She had a change of heart and confessed. Jock Tundell came back."

He laughed. "Jock's a traveller in the rag trade—he brought her back that outfit from Sydney where he'd been all this time. She knew he'd be disappointed if she didn't wear it to Dunedin that day. He'd only got back the weekend before. After the manager told me this I had a word with her and told her I was glad her affairs had got straightened out. I didn't mention her outfit, of course—you made me see it didn't matter, Serena—but she told me herself. She'd been nervous about wearing it and when I didn't mention it that day in Dunedin, thought I hadn't noticed it." He added, "I've given her two weeks off. Thought they ought to go away for a second honeymoon. I'm confident from now on we'll see a difference in her returns."

When he dropped me at the Manse we stopped right under a street light. In its harsh glare his face looked extremely tired and drawn and I spoke without thinking.

"Mr. William, isn't running Durbridge's and Tattoo Bluff too much for you? Doesn't it run you ragged? You look as if you need time off yourself. Why don't you go away for the weekend?"

He said slowly, "I do feel a bit fagged. But I can't this weekend. There's a girl I'm taking out on Saturday to the Maori Kaik. She wants to see the church and the museum section that's at the back of it. She's been in Dunedin for months but has never heard of it. So few Dunedin folk have. And it's well worth a visit.

"Then we're going back to the Bluff to the old coach-house. I told you we had a museum there, didn't I? We've got whaling relics and Maori artifacts. She's doing a project on it." He looked quite mischievous for a moment. I told myself I need waste no sympathy on Master William! He was irrepressible. Sounded like someone from teachers' college. It was completely stupid of me that for one heart-stabbing moment I had felt as if I had really hurt him.

I didn't dare weep. Mother had an eagle eye for such things. She would ask next morning why my eyelids were red. I thought wistfully of the Tundells. Theirs had been a misunderstanding, created by someone who had confessed her part in it. But with me, nobody had made mischief. And I understood that impressionable Mr. William only too well.

CHAPTER NINE

WELL, there was one thing. There were no more scenes between us. But I was dog-tired by Friday night.

Mother said: "Serena, you're going to have your breakfast in bed. I'm having an easy morning myself. Got all the baking done yesterday. Patsy is off with this teacher friend"—she twinkled at me—"they're taking a couple of geography classes up the Maungatuas on a field lesson, and Debbie's off out too, on something similar. You've had too many late nights lately. You've got great shadows under your eyes."

"Yes, Mother," I answered submissively, and groaned inwardly at the thought of lying in bed thinking about Mr. William.

Debbie was all excitement the next morning. She had a new pair of tartan trews on and a red sweater. She came to me in bed and I had to tie her ponytail three times before it suited her.

I said: "For heaven's sake, you aren't going to a party. It's just a class outing, isn't it?"

I was wide awake by this time and decided I'd get up and would shampoo my hair when I showered. Patsy had said to me only last night, "Serena, when you get your hair done next, have them put it back to natural, would you?" She'd giggled. "Alan told me he doesn't like blondes. He's getting a bit mad because I've not let him meet the family yet. But when he does I want you to be your natural self."

Well, I would have the dye taken out, but not quite yet. What a heavenly morning, and since Mother seemed to be so well organised and was only snipping heads off roses, I could be lazy without feeling guilty.

After my hair dried I brushed it and left it loose and retired to the old hammock, strung between the two oaks in the hill garden, to lie in the sun and read. I had a most disreputable sky-blue sweater on and trews that had gone baggy at the knees.

Nice to feel for once just a tomboy, not the impeccable office secretary. I kicked off my flatties and climbed in.

I must have been tired. I woke with a start to the strange feeling of being observed and looked straight up into a pair of sherry-brown eyes.

Mr. William's! And they were laughing. He didn't look in the least like a rejected suitor. Well, he wasn't, at that. He was really courting this Molly as far as serious intentions went. I was just the rather glam girl who wouldn't play ball.

I tried to sit up, but you can't in a hammock. It made me cross. Nothing puts you more at a disadvantage than to be flat on your back, with your hair all over your face and an open book on your chest and—above all—bare feet!

"What on earth are you doing here?" I asked crossly.

"Taking Debbie out. And her pals. I told you. We're going to Otakou, then out to Tattoo Bluff."

"You did *not* say Debbie. You said a girl."

"Oddly enough she does come into that category," he told me, eyes dancing.

"You must have told her not to tell me," I accused.

"No. Wrong way round. *She* told *me* . . . not to tell you."

I felt crosser than ever. "Why?"

"Because you wouldn't like it, she said. Said you had a complex about such things. I thought you probably would have. You have complexes about most things. I find Debbie's conversation both diverting and revealing. She told me you never had liked being too matey with your employers."

"Well, I don't," I said, enraged.

"Now, don't get scotty . . . with me or with Debbie. I'm not asking *you* to come. But Debbie and I had cooked this up before you delivered your final, squashing blow. Well, good morning, my Serene Miss Smith."

I felt like hurling my book after him, but really, a man like that wasn't worth worrying about. He'd taken his congé very lightly. Well, why shouldn't he? He wasn't serious about anyone but Molly.

After they'd gone Mother came up to attack a rambler rose nearby. She looked at me most disapprovingly. "Time that sweater and those trews were thrown out. Fancy your employer seeing you a sight like that!"

I said, "I couldn't care less what he saw me in. After all, my weekends are my own—he only bosses me from Monday to Friday. If you'd wanted me to look like a Paris model—daft and all as it would have been on a Saturday morning—you ought to have said he was taking Debbie out. You didn't tell me on purpose."

"Well, dear, Debbie seemed to think you'd be unpleasant about it, and I do realise you've taken a scunner at the man, so I said nothing. I didn't want Debbie's day spoiled at the outset."

At that moment Father stuck his head out of the window and said, "Serena, my love, seeing you aren't doing anything, would you go down to the church and put these numbers up on the hymn board and leave this list of them beside the organ? Mr. Fellows is going in for a practice at eleven. And this afternoon perhaps you'd run up to Mrs. Wareham's with a couple of books she wants for her Bible Class study?"

What an exciting Saturday! As I went down to get the car out I looked down on the harbour with the masts of the shipping above the wharves, the islands, the countless bays, fringed by the road round which Debbie and her friends and Mr. William would be driving. Later they would go to Tattoo Bluff where no doubt Bunty and Hayley would make a tremendous fuss of them and stuff them with cookies . . . below the house the cliffs would drop down to a sea that would lie like wrinkled blue satin marocain and the odour of sheep would drift up from the empty drafting pens and would sweep in, with intoxicating fragrance, at the windows of the old house. And Debbie would talk ninety to the dozen . . . and heaven knew what about.

For the next week or two I felt I just existed. There

was a sort of hurting pleasure in being with Mr. William in the routine of the office, though even there, with Mrs. Durbridge so much in evidence, it wasn't the same.

Not that she was by any means the martinet she'd been reputed to be. I even said so once to Mr. William, forgetting I was trying to keep everything strictly impersonal.

"I'd rather dreaded the thought of your grand-mother coming back, but considering she was the head of the firm for so long she's not—er—interfering much, is she?"

He said: "No. I've been surprised myself. I wonder if age is creeping up on her. Though—"

"Age? Why, she's much younger than I thought. I mean in her ways."

"Yes, and in her looks. That wasn't what I meant, actually, Miss Smith. At one time the business was her whole life. But now she doesn't seem to be worrying about it and I wondered if she might be losing grip. She was an old warhorse. Yet the other day she said to me: 'William, when I give up the business alto-gether, you don't have to carry it on. When you have a son of your own he might not want to be a draper, and your heart is in the estate.' "

I waited for him to continue, a tightness in my chest. Durbridge's sold? It was unthinkable. Somebody else in Mr. William's chair? Oh, no! I scorned myself for suffering such a stab of pain, but I couldn't help it.

When he returned to his papers I couldn't bear it and said: "And will you?"

"Will I what, Miss Smith? Will I give up the shop? No. And by the way, that was confidential. I wouldn't want any of the staff to feel insecure and get unsettled."

"I won't mention it, Mr. William," I said.

He looked up again. "She was right, of course. I do admire her for changing her ideas on the subject. In the early days she never doubted but that Dad would carry the business on, then after that me, the son she supposed he would have. But she realises now that fewer sons follow their fathers. I don't blame them.

They find they develop their own bent better in a position where they're not under their own father.

"And Gran said, rightly, that many businessmen's sons prefer a profession these days . . . more standing with it. Your professional man is respected more. People think he's got a better mind."

I did feel, vaguely, that he was looking at me hard when he said it, but I was too concerned with my own feelings to analyse it. With the thought that some day, if ever he left the firm, I might have no part in his life at all.

The next day it happened.

Mr. William and his grandmother were in the inner office and one of the girls showed in an American. He was tall and broad with a most good-natured face.

I said : "Is it Mr. William Durbridge or Mrs. Durbridge you would like to see?"

He grinned. "The person I really want to see is Mrs. Bruno P. Harrison."

I stared.

He added : "I guess she's still calling herself Mrs. Durbridge round these parts, the naughty girl, but she definitely is Mrs. Bruno Harrison. She remarried while on a trip to the States."

I tried to take it in.

I said slowly, "What name shall I say?"

And he replied, grinning all over his face, "Why, Bruno P. Harrison, of course!"

He'd said this last in a louder tone, and the next moment the door of the inner office flew open and Mr. William's grandmother was framed in the aperture, Mr. William towering above and behind her.

Bruno P. Harrison gave a great roar and surged across the carpet. "Honey, I just had to come, couldn't stand it a moment longer without you. Thought you'd had time and to spare to get things sorted out here!" Then, accusingly, "You're looking thinner, Laura! I don't like you thin!"

And the next moment he had folded her to him in a bear-hug.

I don't remember ever seeing Mr. William at a loss

before. It was certainly no place for me. I grabbed some papers off my desk and made for the door.

Mrs. Durbridge's voice halted me—I mean Mrs. Harrison's.

"Don't go, Miss Smith. Everyone will have to know now. Bruno, another week or so and I'd have told them."

Bruno chuckled, "Laura, I meant what I said when I said I'd give you a month. I can't do without you, honey, and I don't intend to try to. I can spare a fort-night, then it's back home with me. I've got our flights booked now. I thought you might have felt diffident about telling the family—that any sort of situation might have cropped up, and women go about things in such an oblique way sometimes. Never works. We men just cut through all the red tape.

"This your grandson? I'm sure pleased to meet you, Bill. Laura made you sound just my type. You'd better just call me Bruno, though it would tickle me pink to be Grandpa, mind. We've been married three months. I couldn't get away before. I've got a drygoods store in Texas. We can often fly over here, I tell Laura. New Zealand is a little country I could get mighty fond of. But where I live, Laura lives!"

I gazed at Mrs. Durbridge ... Harrison ... her eyes were sparkling, her slightly lined cheeks carried flakes of carnation pink, her expression was both proud and amused. She liked being bossed. Liked a man who put his foot down.

She said, "It's all right, Bruno, I wasn't stalling. I've been terribly homesick for you. Only—only William seemed—I mean I wanted to get his affairs settled first, then tell him—and there's been this business of Jeff being hurt. I thought he might like to convalesce at Bluff."

"Honey, he can convalesce just as well there, without you. And it will mean we'll be home when he's well enough to fly back to the States." He looked at Mr. William. "Well, you'll be the head of the family on the male side? You'll want to know all about me, I guess?"

Mr. William grinned. "Sure . . . I must find out if you can support my grandmamma in the style to which she's been accustomed. But maybe we can do that at home. Miss Smith, let's see how Mr. Munro is getting on in the reserves with that tally of the sheeting. I think you two could do with a few minutes on your own, then we'll have some tea together."

As he and I walked on to the big office, he hung an 'engaged' placard on the door.

In the reserves he sat down on a bale of blankets and said dazedly, "Well, I'll be darned! Granny!" He looked up at me and said, "I think he's the man for her." Then, "Rather sweet, isn't it? Or does it seem to three-and-twenty, Serena, that marriage so late in life can't possibly be romantic?"

I sat down on another bale, opposite, and said slowly, "I couldn't help looking back as we left the office. Your grandmother was all starry-eyed. I think maybe there was more romance in it than in many young marriages." I added dreamily, "Bunty said that she longed to be mastered, that she had missed being cherished and protected. That all her life she had longed for someone to lean on. That the role of matriarch was thrust upon her was what Bunty meant, I suppose. So perhaps this is a dream come true for your grandmother. Oh, I do hope no one rubs the bloom off. Mr. William, do you think you could ring Bunty and tell her in case she says anything that might?"

I knew Mr. William could see I had tears in my eyes.

Mr. Jennings came through the fixtures and halted out of sheer amazement seeing his chief and secretary sitting on the blanket bales under the great light well. We both shot to our feet.

"We're recovering from shock, Malcolm," said Mr. William. "You won't believe this, but my grandmother's husband, her brand-new, American husband, has just arrived in the office. They were married two months ago—no, three, wasn't it, Serena? He's a draper too. She's going back with him in a fortnight's time, and no hanky-panky about it either. I can't take it in myself.

Look, Malcolm, you'd better come and meet him. Miss Smith and I walked out on them to give them a chance of a few moments alone together. I've an idea I'm going to like Bruno P. Harrison very much indeed."

Everybody did. Of course it caused a terrific flutter right through the shop. Laura Harrison took him through the departments, introducing him. She told them all that she would be going back to the States to live but that Durbridge's would be carrying on as usual, under Mr. William.

I thought Mr. William still had a dazed air as he set off with the two of them for Tattoo Bluff.

I went off to have my hair done. I was getting it restored to its original colour at night so that I could get used to it again myself.

Patsy was bringing her teacher home this weekend. I felt a bit sick and scared about it. All I could hope was that he would look at my hair without an atom of admiration.

Yet when it was finished I was glad to be a shining, pale gold again. With mouse-coloured locks I'd often looked at my reflection and felt I faced a stranger.

The hairdresser was scornful of whatever had prompted me to dye my hair. I passed it off as lightly as possible. "Like all girls I wanted a change."

"Well, it certainly wasn't one for the better," she said.

I tried to subdue all thought of Mr. William and his reaction to the change by keeping my mind on the fact that there were going to be some odd comments the next day in the staff-room. They'd think it was dyed *now*.

So I felt very flat when, having survived the barrage in the cloakroom, with everyone saying I must have been clean mad to have dyed it and some still sceptical that this *was* my own colouring, Mr. William came in when I was already seated at my desk and merely said : "Oh, very nice. Your hair, I mean."

He went out later and his grandmother arrived in, Bruno P. Harrison in tow. No, that wasn't quite right . . . he was too much the man of affairs to be in tow to anyone. He was like a big, blustery wind, warm-hearted, genial, a man who would make for very good Kiwi-American relations.

He stopped short as he caught sight of me. "Well, Miss Serena Smith, you've gone blonde. It sure looks nice. Laura, you ought to get a chestnut rinse."

She laughed, looked at me in the most friendly fashion and said, quite gently, "But it's your natural colour, isn't it, Serena?"

It was the first time she had called me anything but Miss Smith.

I nodded.

Bruno looked staggered. "Now, honey, what would a girl be wanting to dye hair that colour for?"

Laura's smile was as one woman to another. "Serena had a bit of bother with her former bosses. Blondes do. I think she must have taken William for a wolf too, so took no chances. Not that it made an atom of difference. It would take more than mousy hair to make you anything less than a beauty, Serena. Well, you can really let yourself go now. I've summed you up. You aren't a money-chasing, man-mad hussy. Quite the contrary. I think I nearly scared the life out of you, pouncing on you and William. I'd heard about that Veronica, you see. But that wasn't serious at all. You know that, don't you? Nothing for you to worry about."

She looked at me expectantly, her head on one side like a bright-eyed bird. I felt horribly embarrassed. She couldn't know about Molly. Or was it that she did but didn't suspect she was anything more than the girl-next-door to Mr. William?

I said hurriedly, "Mrs. Durbridge... I mean Mrs. Harrison... I'd better tell you the real reason I dyed my hair. A man my sister was in love with transferred his attentions to me. I felt horrible. Patsy and I had been such pals. I vowed it would never happen again, so became mouse. Unfortunately she tumbled to it. She got over the other affair, fell in love again. She demanded I put my hair back to its original colour. She's bringing him home this weekend."

Bruno P. Harrison reached out a big hand and patted my high-piled golden hair. "I like this little girl, don't you, Laura?"

He really was a sweetie. And I liked being called little. Tall people do. Because you know they use the diminutive out of sheer affection.

The next night was Friday night, and about seven-thirty Mr. William sent me down to the hosiery department with a message for the head. Coming back through the men's department I ran slap bang into Patsy and her friend. It looked so domestic. They were buying him a shirt.

Patsy got a shock when recognition was mutual. I cried, "Why, Alan Burford, for goodness' sake! Are *you* the chap my little sister has been going round with? Well, fancy it being you!"

Alan said, "Well, the way she's been keeping me a secret you probably thought there was something peculiar about me. I'd like to have met your people weeks ago." He turned to Patsy. "Serena and I were at Auckland Varsity together, then I actually worked for the firm she did, during the long vacation. In fact two or three vacations. But I never associated you with her. Smith is such an anonymous sort of name. I believe now I did hear Serena's father was a minister, but I'd forgotten it till now. Well, I won't feel half so badly running the gauntlet of the family tomorrow. You might even persuade your father that I'm not a bad sort of chap. I was getting a bit browned off at not meeting them. If I had met them by now, Patsy and I might have been shopping for a ring tonight, but I must see your father first."

Patsy was all starry-eyed. I looked from one to the other. "Truly?" I felt delighted. I added: "Well, it's no more than a formality. Dad would expect us to choose our own mates. I feel sure you'll be able to shop for that ring on Monday after school. Patsy, how clever of you to pick on Alan. I'll feel it's no stranger being introduced into the family circle."

I didn't dare say to her to tell Alan why she'd

hesitated. Patsy might not want him to know about Mark. I certainly wouldn't embarrass her by dragging it up.

At midnight that night she came into my room, bent over me in the concealing darkness and said, kissing me, "Thank you, Serena. I could giggle madly or cry or something. Months of keeping your hair mouse . . . and it turned out Alan had known you when you were dazzlingly blonde and had never once tried to date you. God bless, darling, and thank you for the sacrifice." She paused, added, "But perhaps it will have its compensations. Your nice William Durbridge will love you twice as much gold as mouse."

I struggled up, alarmed, and said in a firm tone, "Patsy Smith! You're absolutely nuts! Mr. William and I mean absolutely nothing to each other!"

But she was still laughing as she went through to her room. Of course people in love themselves always wanted everyone else to be in love too.

Earlier that night a toll-call had come through at the shop for Mr. William from his sister in Christchurch. Jeff had been out of hospital a week and at the motel, we knew, but now they were all coming down to Tattoo Bluff for Jeff to convalesce there.

What a happy family reunion there would be. With Jeff's mother there it would be very pleasant for Bruno P. Harrison. And the Smiths would be celebrating what was practically an engagement. It seemed to be the time for happy endings. But not mine.

The family loved Alan Burford. Mother said to Patsy when we were doing the dishes Saturday night, "We ought to have met him months ago. But Serena said you didn't wish to have us take things for granted."

Patsy kissed her. "Well, it could scare any chap off . . . her family looking on him as inevitably her husband." She winked at me over Mother's unsuspecting shoulder. She added: "It looks as if you'll be back to a hen with one chick soon, Mother. Just Debbie left."

"Just Debbie?" I looked at Patsy as if I thought she'd gone mad. "What ever do you mean? *I'm* still heart-whole and fancy-free."

She and Mother exchanged wicked looks, and Patsy said : "Are you, Serena?" in a tone of great surprise.

I said hastily, "I know what you're thinking. You know, Patsy, you were right. Families *are* embarrassing. Especially sisters so head over heels in love that they can't imagine everyone else isn't in the same blissful state ! Just because Lance came down from Auckland it doesn't mean he's in love with me. After all, if he'd decided he was going in for the ministry, he'd have to come here to the theological hall at Knox College. It's the only Presbyterian one in New Zealand—as you know."

"Very clever !" said Patsy, her pansy-brown eyes alight with laughter. "If that had been what I was referring to, I could knock that argument into a cocked hat, my darling sister. After all, it will be two years before Lance can get into the theological hall and he could have gone on with varsity work at Auckland just the same. But who said I was talking about Lance Reedway? I was talking—"

But I had gone. They could finish the dishes themselves.

At three-thirty the next afternoon the door-bell went and Debbie answered it. The next moment she was coming into the living-room, leading Mr. William by the hand.

"Here he is," she said clearly, with the air of a conjuror producing an outsize rabbit from his hat.

"I'm very glad to be He with a capital H," said Mr. William.

Well, for once I wasn't wearing what Mother called one of my unspeakable jerseys. I felt quite elegant in an oatmeal suit with a jerkin jacket and a chunky wooden necklace that Dad had brought back from one of the Pacific Islands when he'd been on a missionary survey. Not that it mattered, of course. Mr. William was nothing in my private life.

Mother began pouring him a cup of tea. "You can't have had your afternoon tea yet because it would take you an hour to come in from Tattoo Bluff. Sandwich or nut loaf?"

Mr. William looked at me and I could have sworn there was an appeal in his eye for me not to turn him down in front of all the family.

He sounded quite apologetic, for him. "Kitty insisted that I come and get you, Serena. She was so grateful to you for looking after Wilhelmina that week, and vows she was so preoccupied when we went up to Christchurch that she didn't thank you properly. And Granny thought it would be nice too, to say nothing of Bruno. He's fallen for you in a big way. Besides, Wilhelmina just can't understand you not being there. She thinks you belong to Tattoo Bluff. Any chance of coming? I wanted to ring you to find how you were situated, but Kitty vowed if I did you'd say it was too far for me to come to get you or some such nonsense. It really would give Kitty and Jeff pleasure if you would come."

With the eyes of the entire family upon me I just couldn't be churlish. I meekly went to get my bag and gloves.

It was a true late April day. By next week the flaming colours of autumn would be fading. The russet and gold leaves would be beginning to release their hold on the branches, but now the cherry trees were brick and coral, the golden ash translucently pale, the poplars like flaming torches among the sombre pines and firs, the larches and the birches masses of quivering gold, and the sea at Waitati as we neared Blueskin Bay had its Sunday look, which was according to Debbie, who always vowed it shimmered more on Sundays.

As we swept in past the old-fashioned coach-house I had a feeling once more that I had come home...I who, because of Daddy being a minister, had never struck roots anywhere. This in spite of the fact that Mr. William had been so silent, even taciturn, on the way out.

He'd said: "I couldn't get out of this, Serena. I don't want you to think me unbearably persistent. But the family have no idea that we've been at logger-heads. I want Gran to go away feeling easy in her mind about the shop and she knows you are an efficient secretary. So let's play it that way, will you? They'll all be away soon and it won't matter."

I'd said, just as matter-of-factly, "Yes, I quite under-stand you couldn't get out of this today. I was more or less pitchforked into your affairs that weekend Kitty flew here. And I do like Kitty. I'll quite enjoy meeting her again."

Then I wished it unsaid. It sounded as if I liked Kitty but not her brother. And liking ... or loving ... didn't come into it. It was a matter of not being able to trust him.

I wondered that Mrs. Harrison could bear to leave this home, set in its jewel-bright gardens above a sapphire sea, with the faint pink cliffs of Waikouiti in the north, circling round. She had lived here fifty years. Yet she was as eager as a girl about leaving for the States. For her, in the evening of her life, a dream had come true. I hoped they might have many years together.

When she looked back, would she wish she had met Bruno earlier?—That they had known the spring, the greening and the gold, together. Instead of just late autumn?

Would *I* ever find my dreams come true? For most girls their dearest wish was to find their ideal man. Some settled for a lot less. Maybe it was stupid to want an ideal. But at least, in marriage, you needed to trust your husband. Besides, Mr. William didn't think of marriage in connection with me. Only with Molly.

Wilhelmina tumbled over herself in her eagerness to kiss me. It dispelled all stiffness. Jeff was walking with a stick and his hair was all uneven lengths where it had been shaved off, but he was an exceedingly handsome man. Kitty had lost her brittle look and was just a girl. Sad to think this affectionate family would soon be scattered again. Bruno, you could see, was a great favourite with Wilhelmina.

Hayley was at her own house again, for Bunty was mobile now and had Kitty to help her. I so loved Bunty. Best of all. She was austere and forbidding, but you knew where you were with her. She either liked you or didn't. I went out with her into the kitchen for a yarn.

"I'd ha' thought you'd ha' been out here long since," she said.

I said I'd been busy.

Bunty said, her eyes fixed on mine, "Did *she* upset you?" She jerked her head towards the big drawing-room. "Mrs. Durbridge ... I mean Harrison? Never worry about her first reception of you—she thought you were that Veronica that daft lad of mine was rushing for a while. Really, the way he goes on! But don't let him worry you. He'll settle down, you'll see."

I turned pink. I don't know who invented blushing, but it's a devilish thing.

Bunty observed it and chuckled in her rusty way. "I'm putting my foot in it, which is what I do times without number, but it's time Bill settled down. He's nearly thirty. This house will need a new mistress. And I think he himself is ready now to settle. You'd do me."

I got up hastily, smiled at her uncertainly and said, "Bunty, there isn't anything like that between us ... it's just wishful thinking on your part because you and I—clicked. It's awfully sweet of you, but—well, we just aren't suited to each other." I ran back to the big room.

Just as I entered there was the sound of hoof-beats outside.

Mr. William looked out of the window nearest him and his face lit up. "It's Molly!" he exclaimed, and went out of the room saying, "I didn't know she was back."

He came in with an arm round her shoulder. Her riding habit fitted as if she had been poured into it and her lovely nut-brown hair was as glossy as a lark's wing or a polished acorn. She had a wild-rose complexion.

A girl of the outdoors, yet so well-groomed. What a chatelaine she would make for Tattoo Bluff.

They all rushed to kiss her. Molly sat down and presently Wilhelmina was astride one breeched leg, being jogged up and down. The child had taken to her immediately. I was amazed at the wave of jealousy that swept over me. How ridiculous, to be jealous over the affections of a two-year-old! But you've never been in love before, my heart reminded my mind.

The girl next door was right ... even if that appellation meant five miles away. Seemingly once it had been all one estate, but part had been sold, and Molly's people's place was called Moko Point. Moko was Maori for Tattoo. Their links would be strong, forged through the years.

Molly stayed for the evening meal and darkness came down, so Mr. William wouldn't allow her to ride back. "You can stable Jasper here and stay the evening and I'll run you back home. Bruno can run Serena back." (Wonder he didn't call me Miss Smith ... it was quite evident he wanted Molly to know she had prior claim on him, that I was only his secretary, that I wouldn't have been here had not his sister wanted to thank me properly.) I felt dreary.

But I was glad when Wilhelmina wanted *me* to bath her and to hear her prayers. I had her to myself. As I tucked her up in bed, rosy, cosy, and clean, smelling of baby powder and sweetly drowsy, I looked down on her and noticed how like Mr. William she was. She could have been his daughter. She could have been mine. Ours.

I dropped a kiss on the sunny curls and went downstairs. I didn't think I could stand much more of the evening. So I got Bruno to take me home in the other car. As we said goodbye at the door of the drawing-room I carried away the picture of Mr. William sitting on the arm of Molly's chair, showing her some coloured photos of Kitty and Jeff's home. Well, it was what I wanted, wasn't it?—For him to leave me alone.

It wasn't till I was dropping off to sleep that I realised why Molly seemed hauntingly familiar ... she was the girl who had been at the film that night—with a very handsome escort—and who'd been talking to Veronica and William. I couldn't understand it. Or had Molly done it deliberately? Gone out with someone else to make Mr. William jealous? It could be.

Oh, Serena, go to sleep, he's not for you.

CHAPTER TEN

MRS. BRUNO HARRISON drove herself in next morning. As she came into the office, stripping off her gloves with the quick, nervy gestures that were individually hers, she said, passing me, "Mr. William isn't coming in this morning. He's spending the day at Tattoo."

I said feebly, "I suppose he needs to once in a while."

"Yes, he often does, but I don't expect he did much while I was away. Got a strong sense of duty, that lad. And he's riding Jasper over for Molly. Her father will run him back. Or Molly. He and Molly's father have a lot in common, besides boundaries. And Hubert was away in Australia and William hasn't seen him since he got back."

I got on with my work. The phone rang. It was the Waitati exchange, so my heart began beating a tattoo. It would be my boss.

It was. "That you, Serena?" Just the ordinary friendly tone he'd used to me ever since that night at Lake Waihola. Nothing like the tone he had used to me when he was in Christchurch with Kitty. And that wasn't imagination, it was fact.

He said: "I've done an awful thing—forgotten Molly's birthday. I'm not riding over there till this afternoon, so I wondered if you could choose something for me and send it out and she'd never know I'd forgotten. It could come out on the late morning bus. Can do? Good girl! Look, Serena, I want to be quite sure I get it; I know it's making an errand girl of you, but how about you taking it to the Road Services Bus Depot yourself? Thanks, I knew I could depend on you."

I said, "Mr. William, what would you suggest?"

"Oh, get something from the shop. That would be the easiest, and apart from jewellery we've got about everything. I wonder how about a tea-set. Oh, no, I can't take that over on Jasper. Look, can't I leave it to you?"

I toyed madly with the idea of saying : "What about a stole, the same as you gave Veronica?" but thought I'd better not go too far—but I'd have loved to have underlined the fact that I knew he was playing fast and loose with the two of them.

I suggested gloves, nylons, a bag. None of them found favour. He ummmed and aahed for a few moments, then said, "I know ... pick out some really choice lingerie out of those new samples in the buying room. There's an apricot set that would be ravishing with her hair and ... oh, I'll leave the rest to you. Say two sets, including negligées. Trousseau stuff. That ought to thrill her. Get the dispatch department to wrap it. Miles of tissue paper and fancy gift paper, true lovers' knots and all the doings ... satin ribbon and whatnot. Type out a card, "Love to Molly from Bill" and on your way pick up a box of flowers from Florista's. If you ring them now they'll have them made up when you call. Stocks and roses and carnations, say. Thanks a lot, Serena, I knew I could rely on you."

And he hung up.

Well, I'd wanted him to treat me that way. Just as an employee. I'd been right in turning him down. Nothing went deeply with Mr. William.

I had to explain where I was going, to his grandmother. I didn't think she was over-pleased. "My word, he's changed. He'll be half the day running after her. He works too hard. And he's had so many distractions of late. Oh, well, if those are his orders I can scarcely countermand them. Though I'll be glad of your services as soon as you can get back, Serena."

I made myself choose the most exquisite of all the sets. I chose white for the other one. I supposed it ought to be a bridal one. I found the whole thing ironic.

I wouldn't let myself even start to imagine what it would be like to receive such a gift from Mr. William, knowing he loved you. No use turning the sword.

I got it on to the bus and came thankfully back to tackle more work. But my thoughts were at Tattoo Bluff.

I had the sense of time running out. It was most odd. I felt as if I didn't want Mr. William's grandmother to go back to the States. Though I couldn't think why.

Unless I thought that with his grandmother gone from the old home he might be more likely to want to settle down with a wife of his own. I made a few mistakes that day I was ashamed of and finished up by taking work home to make up for it.

Bruno Harrison changed his bookings. He got them transferred to a week later. When the date was definitely fixed Mr. William and the heads of the departments got their heads together and decided they'd give Laura Harrison a farewell dinner. I saw Mr. William's flair for organisation in action and marvelled at it.

I also saw how eager and enthusiastic his staff was to back him up in such things. I even curled my lip about it a little, which was horrible of me, but I put it down once more to personal charm. I told myself that it suited him to turn it on like a tap.

The tea-rooms were doing the dinner. They kept it from Mrs. Harrison till the Friday night when she had to be told because Mr. William realised she was making a counter-arrangement. Bruno was in the office at the time. Laura Harrison looked absolutely surprised. "A farewell dinner for me? You say the staff suggested it, not you, William?"

He nodded. "It was Miss Buckingham's idea really and the others took it up with great gusto. There are to be guests from outside too. From wholesale firms, from the other retail firms." He turned and said to me, "I've asked Lance Reedway, Serena. Gran knew Mrs.

Reedway in business, so I thought he could represent some of the Auckland firms. He won't know many down here, bar some of the travellers, but you could look after him."

I could have choked him. I was seeing as little of Lance as possible. He still came to the Manse and seemed awfully fond of Father, who always had an interest in divinity students, of course, but I'd told him I didn't want to put myself in a false position by going out with him.

He'd taken it very well, and because of that (because once he had been a spoilt son) I realised how much more there was to him now. His world had broadened. Strange how I never thought Mr. William's world needed broadening. But then he wasn't under his grandmamma's thumb as Lance had been under his mother's. As far as Lance was concerned, though it had been I who had jolted him out of his rut, I felt I'd served my turn. That it would be some other girl who would finally hold his heart, capturing it as I had never done. I'd just been an instrument. I didn't think any man was ever likely to pine away for love of me. Mr. William had taken my rejection of him very lightly. They only fell in love with my looks, not the real me.

However, Lance was delighted to be accompanying me. I was flummoxed when I found that Mr. William had invited Mother and Father, Patsy and Alan, even Debbie.

"He's invited *Debbie*?" I said at the table when they told me.

Debbie looked enraged. "Why not? Me and Mr. William—I mean I and Mr. William—are kindred spirits. We're twin souls. We both love artifacts . . . adzes and fish-hooks and bone needles and Maori meanings and shells and—"

"All right, all right," I muttered, "spare me a list of his virtues. To you folk he's a charming man. To me he's just my boss, and I never meant to have my family so mixed up with my business life. It's like walking on a volcano!"

But I relented to the extent of buying Debbie a frock

that took her breath away. Debbie was as blonde as I was, but with the right sort of eyes . . . sapphire blue, not like mine, brown, with green specks. So the frock was blue and came from Durbridge's Teenage Department, which, as Debbie had just turned twelve, delighted her.

It even gave her immature figure a slight fullness. It was cleverly swathed in the bodice. I saw Father watching her with a bemused look as she pirouetted round, the full skirt swinging out in perfect union with her ponytail, as if he doubted this lovely creature could be his. I suddenly found myself praying that when Debbie fell in love it might be all joy, not heartbreak. Nothing to rub off the dew.

Debbie said, smoothing the skirt down each side, "I feel like Deborah, not Debbie, in this. That's what I like about Mr. William, he always calls me Deborah."

I hardly saw Mr. William that Monday morning, he was so busy arranging things for the dinner. He gave me a plan of the main table, neatly marked in with names, and asked me to type the place cards for them.

Mr. William was to be seated on his grandmother's left. On *his* left was Molly Raeburn and next to her her mother and father. It was as near as that! Practically settled. Would an engagement be announced between them soon? A horrible thought struck me. They might do it tonight, deem it a fitting function.

I was glad to get out of the shop in my dinner-hour. I wandered along George Street, lifted my eyes to Mount Cargill, and wished passionately that I could take a quick run up there, to stand on the hill top and feel the winds of God against my face, the tang of the salt air . . . to know the lifting of the heart that only solitude could bring.

Solitude . . . I looked across the street to where the gracious steeple of Knox Church rose almost from the street. I love a church that rises up from the heart of commerce. God where He is meant to be . . . in the midst of His people.

There would be solitude there, and peace. I was finding it increasingly hard to be at peace with myself.

I crossed the street, went in at the corner gate, found the door open as usual, pushed open the inner door and went into the semi-gloom and stillness of the great church.

I had eyes only for the stained glass window arched above the communion table. Christ in all His Majesty. There was a knot of people at the far end, probably tourists, and two or three people knelt in the pews. I slipped into a back seat and knelt too.

Something I'd heard Dad quote once came into my mind ... "Every prayer that rises from the heart leaves more room there for God."

At first I found it hard to pray. Then a change took place within me and I knew that I'd find the grace to accept it ... I found myself praying that Mr. William would find happiness and that he would be a constant husband.

I rose, feeling a different person from the one who had come in, and turned to the centre aisle to come out.

And found myself facing Mr. William.

He'd come out of the opposite pew. I realised now that his must have been that dim figure that knelt there when I came in.

Normally, returning to the everyday world from a deep experience, I'd have felt embarrassed. I was surprised to find I wasn't.

He spoke first, gravely, not smiling. "I like a church that keeps its doors open for people to pray in, Serena."

"So do I, Mr. William. Even if one must risk—and sometimes suffer—vandalism."

"Yes ... better to replace furnishings than for anyone who needed comfort to find a closed door." He added : "Do you often come here in your dinner-hour?"

I said, "I've only been once or twice since working at Durbridge's. Do you?"

"Not in my dinner-hour. But always before work Monday mornings. However, I had to take the car in to be serviced this morning. I always find there are more staff upsets Monday mornings than any other time and sometimes I'm less fitted to deal with them then. I'm often a little edgy myself then, facing another week of the shop after a glorious weekend at Tattoo Bluff. I find it helps."

We had come to the door.

He said, "I've got to pick the car up now." He pointed north.

I said, "And I've got to get a buckle for Deborah's hair. She's allowed to have it up tonight. See you later, Mr. William."

I felt comforted, at peace.

I would always treasure that memory. I'd put it away between wisps of lavender. And it helped me through that interminable dinner, those endless speeches, with Molly, looking like an Irish colleen in vivid green, her nut-brown hair a lovely contrast to Mr. William's closely cropped dark head, sitting beside him.

And I, just a staff member.

Well, wasn't that what I'd wanted to be?

So I was most surprised when I was invited to a family dinner at the homestead on the Wednesday night. Mrs. Harrison asked me and I couldn't think of an excuse. I might have, had Mr. William done the asking.

To my look of surprise she said, "Kitty is very set on it. I don't think you'll feel out of it, because we don't look on you as just an employee, you know. You came to Kitty's rescue when she was desperately pressed for time." She added: "I don't remember my grandson ever having a secretary like you before, combining charm and efficiency and with it all never presuming. Some girls, more or less pitchforked into the bosom of the family, as you were, would have taken advantage of it. You haven't. Thank you, Serena."

It would have been ungracious to refuse. I rang Kitty and asked her what to wear. I didn't want to be either under-dressed or over-dressed.

Kitty was sweet. "I ought to have told Gran to tell you. She and my brother will be bringing you out, so perhaps you'd like to change here. Just semi-evening dress, Serena. Gran loves occasions, belongs to the old school. For instance, she'll never countenance me sitting down to dinner in slacks, but has no objection to me changing into them afterwards. It's an occasion for the 'little black', Serena. I don't mean literally, but—"

I laughed. "That's just what it will have to be. I don't want to wear what I wore the other night. I've got a black lace over oyster satin . . . just a plain sheath style."

But it suited me, I knew. Kitty thought so too. She'd put Wilhelmina's room at my disposal. I'd showered and changed and felt like a giant refreshed.

There was something about round tables . . . well, with the leaves in, it was oval. Somehow more communal. It was cool enough for a fire and the leaping flames were reflected in the polished panelling.

"Driftwood?" I asked Mr. William, looking at a log burning with sulphur-yellow, copper-green, will o' the wisp blue.

He nodded. "Yes, Gran loves a driftwood fire, so I went down the cliff this morning for this."

I tried to keep my mind off the thought of some day Mr. William sitting with his wife here, in front of this very fireplace, watching driftwood flames, sitting hand in hand.

I said : "I thought Molly would have been here." My voice didn't even shake a little. That quiet five minutes in Knox Church had given me confidence and strength. I would see this thing through to the bitter end, even to seeing Mr. William married to Molly if that was his heart's desire.

Mr. William said : "Molly's in Christchurch again. She'll say goodbye to Bruno and Gran at the airport."

Jeff was looking very fit. Wilhelmina had grown a whole inch since she had come to New Zealand, her mother told me. Kitty was radiant. Jeff's mother was a lovable person. I felt sad that soon all these lovely people would be gone out of my life. No doubt Kitty would come home sometimes to see her brother, but her life was in the States as was her grandmother's now. And I felt I'd miss Bruno most of all. He was so spontaneous, so natural, so boyish for his age. No wonder Laura Durbridge had fallen in love with him.

Then there was the bitter-sweet of the drive home with Mr. William, across the motorway that was folded in the valley by the dark, clustering hills, then rose up through the plantations of larch and fir to dip down to the sequin-studded shadows of the city.

There, along George Street, was Durbridge's, its neon sign lighting and flashing.

"Are you going in to get your grandmother's ring now, Mr. William?" I asked. She had discovered she had left it in the office that afternoon when she had been trying on gloves she had had sent up from the department. She'd asked Mr. William to go in to retrieve it.

"It's an idea," he said. "It's fairly late and the time clock will switch the lights off soon and I forgot a torch. Like to come in with me? I don't like you sitting alone outside. Some odd bods round in a city at night."

There was enough light from the windows and the front departments to light us to the stairs. "We'll take the front ones," said Mr. William in a low voice scarcely more than a whisper. Big deserted buildings have that effect on you.

I didn't feel like talking anyway. I wanted to savour just being alone with Mr. William, it so scarcely happened these days.

We reached the mantles and our feet sank into the luxurious carpeting. The department looked very spooky as we began to cross it. All the racks and stands had dust sheets thrown over them and the models on the island display stands had been swathed in muslin so that they looked like drowned Ophelias in the green light that came from a neon sign on the opposite building. I instinctively drew nearer Mr. William and he put a hand under my elbow.

We were halfway across when we heard it. A faint, metallic sound from the office! We stopped dead in our tracks, listening with all our might. For the first few moments I couldn't hear anything for the thudding of my heart and the drumming of my pulses. Then my senses steadied. I expect Mr. William was experiencing the same thing.

His hand closed round my upper arm and his other hand came across my lips. He needn't have worried. I wasn't going to make a sound.

We heard noises, definitely metal noises, and whispers.

Mr. William turned me round and we tiptoed back to the head of the stairs, where he paused. He bent and said in my ear on just a thread of sound, "They must be after the safe. Serena, can you go extremely quietly out into the street, drawing the door shut behind you so it won't bang ... and get help? Stop the first man you see—but not louts—or stop a car. Get them to get the police. If the street is deserted ring the police. *And then stay out of it.*"

I reached up my arms to his neck and pulled his head down to me so I could reach his ear. "Yes, will do ... but promise me you won't tackle them till I get help."

He whispered back, "I'll just keep watch—to see where they go if they hear anything. Now, no noise."

I bent down and wrenched off my sling-back shoes. Those tiny heels might give a resonant tap when I reached the downstairs floor. Next moment I was running down the stairs and across the ground floor. There was but one thought in my mind ... to get help before Mr. William did anything. It had not escaped me that he had made no promise.

It was a wonderful feeling to be out in the street and to feel that help for him was that much nearer. I thought he was sensible enough not to crash in on them unless he had to, but still—

I vaguely noticed the small stones on the pavement that hurt my feet, but they didn't matter. Luck was with me. I saw a good broadly-built man just a few yards up the street. He stopped in amazement as an elegantly dressed female without shoes charged towards him.

I clutched him. "There are burglars in the office at Durbridge's. Mr. Durbridge is up there watching them.

I'm his secretary. Will you get the police? The second door from here, behind the island windows, is open. I'll wedge it. Tell them to make as little noise as possible because they'll be cornered more easily in the office if they don't get disturbed." (I thought afterwards, what a nerve . . . teaching the police their business!)

He went into instant action. "There's a policeman on his rounds in the next block. I'll send him and do the phoning myself."

I fled back, my heart in my mouth. I put a heavy chair against the door for a quick entrance by the police and fled to the stairs.

I made good speed up them and gained the showroom. I mustn't bump into anything now and give the show away. Not till someone got here. I felt Mr. William wouldn't have been able to resist getting as near the office as he could. He wouldn't be prepared for me coming back, so I mustn't run into him.

But I had taken only about half a dozen cautious steps when pandemonium broke out. I somehow knew Mr. William was in the thick of it. I ran, shouting at the top of my voice, "We're coming, sir, we're coming!"

It is odd how at times like that one acts instinctively and afterwards can't remember the sequence. I must have grabbed a steel T-stand and wrenched the coat off it. The office door was open and figures were grappling by it. It was like seeing a crime film that was too dark on a television set. There were dark forms and grunts and thuds as fists hit flesh.

They were near the door, and that gave me my chance. I charged into the dark mass of figures, staggering them a bit, and snapped the lights on.

Just as they came on Mr. William knocked one man flying, but another man—whom presumably he'd cracked a moment before—was pushing himself up against the wall to attack again. Mr. William hadn't noticed this and was intent on further punishing his present opponent and lunged forward.

As the second man ran at him, I did the only thing I could think of, put my head down and charged him like a bull. I can still remember with amazement and perhaps a little bit of guilt the thrill of exaltation that ran over me as he crashed over the wastepaper basket.

I heard Mr. William shout "Bravo, Serena!" as he grabbed the other man by the shoulders. I dimly realised there was a third man there, simply leaning against the wall, with cash bags in his hand, but he seemed dazed . . . or else I was.

The man closed with Mr. William. Mr. William was built squarely, all bone and muscle and a terrific reach. Mr. William picked him up, then dumped him on the floor with such force it must have knocked all the breath out of him, but unfortunately the impetus carried Mr. William on and he tripped and went clean over the fellow's head.

In the excitement I'd forgotten the man I'd charged, and he came at me again. I yelled and swung my T-stand out in front of me in a tremendous arc that swept him back. He was swearing furiously, and now I noticed, incredulously, that they all had nylons over their faces, giving them a weird, featureless look.

I was most apprehensive about that third man. If he joined in, we were done for. The man under Mr. William must have got his breath back and he heaved just as Mr. William was struggling to his feet. I dropped my T-stand and grabbed the man's legs.

But the man made a convulsive heave with his body and Mr. William hadn't gained his balance and fell back, face upwards. To my complete horror I saw the other man, with a huge paperweight in his hand, raise his arm to strike Mr. William.

If only I hadn't let go that stand! I grabbed it, yelled: "Get back, you . . . get back!" and just as he brought the weight down on Mr. William's head, I swung at him, clean at his face, and to my fancy, the two blows landed at once and I was almost sure I had been too late.

The man collapsed over Mr. William, the force of my swing took me clean across them and I landed on all fours, striking my temple on Mrs. Harrison's desk.

At that moment there was a thud and a grunt from nearer the door, and a "Got you!" That was the police-

man with the man with the cash-bags. He'd collared
him. I managed to look round as I scrambled up.

The loveliest sight I'd ever seen ... or ever would
see ... a navy blue uniform with shining buttons. Then
there was the wonderful sound of reinforcements charg-
ing upstairs. No need for silence now.

I hardly knew what was happening in detail. Only
that first civilians, then more police arrived. The man
I'd commandeered had roped in others as he sped
back from the telephone ... leather-jacketed boys, a
couple of American sailors from the Antarctic picket-
ship in port, a quite elderly man.

It was soon over then. The man I'd hit with the
T-stand was lying quite still, but I had no eyes for him.
Because so was Mr. William. It looked as if I had swung
a second too late. If only I hadn't dropped the stand
to grab that man's legs! Mr. William had a great
bruise on his temple and blood at his mouth.

I pulled his head on to my lap. I looked up as the
policeman dragged the stockings off the face of the
man who'd had the bags and a wave of nausea went
over me, and I gasped: "Oh, no! Mr. Rasmorton,
Mr. Rasmorton!"

The sergeant whipped round. "You know him?"

I said, through shaking lips, "Know him? He's our
accountant ... a trusted employee. Durbridge's accountant. I can't believe it!"

I looked down at Mr. William's unconscious face
against my breast and said, "This is Mr. William
Durbridge. I'm his secretary." And I looked straight at
Mr. Rasmorton. He met my eyes for one sickening,
shaming second and dropped them.

The sergeant grunted. "Very clever. Opened it with
your key and your pals had explosives to use afterwards, to make it look like an outside job. Not that
it would have made much difference. We'd have
worked it out. What do you think the police are?
Fools?"

I said urgently, "Can we get a doctor here, quick?"
Then, agonisingly, "Oh, he's bleeding at the mouth.
Has he fractured his skull?"

One policeman dropped down beside me, pulled Mr. William's lips away from his teeth. "No, he's just cut his lip badly . . . inside the mouth. It's all right, lady, he's probably just concussed."

The policeman who'd been first on the scene said with a chuckle, "But you've certainly knocked his opponent out cold. Never saw such a blow or such an effective weapon. What an Amazon! You ought to join the police force. Ever thought of it?" He added: "It would have been a mighty lot worse if you hadn't deflected his aim."

I said gratefully, "Oh, do you really think so? I was terrified I'd only added weight to it."

"Not a bit of it. I saw it from the side. If it had been delivered the way he intended to, he'd be in very bad shape." He never knew how near he came to being kissed. Though nothing really mattered to me while Mr. William lay there pallid and uncaring.

I moved my arm and saw a great dark patch of blood on Mr. William's coat. I don't know what I said, but suddenly the policeman was holding my arm and saying, "That's not his blood—it's yours. You've gashed your arm." He looked at the base of the T-stand. "I reckon you cut your arm on that when the force of your swing took you over them."

It hadn't hurt till then. I told them where the first-aid kit in the office was. "I can't go on bleeding all over Mr. William."

Out in the street we heard the wail of the ambulance.

The man I'd clocked was taken off in the same ambulance and they let me sit beside Mr. William. A policeman went with us and another one was beside the driver and his assistant. The man I'd press-ganged into helping us came along too. He didn't want to miss a moment. It was the biggest thrill of his life. I tried to thank him.

Not till I got to hospital did I realise the mess I was in. I hadn't picked up my shoes, my hair was streaming over my face, and the neck of my lace frock was ripped. I kept trying to hold it up. The civilian gave me a couple of pins from his lapel.

Both men lay so still it filled me with dread. My teeth were beginning to chatter from shock. But nothing really mattered except that Mr. William was out to it. Later on I might begin to be concerned about that other man because I was the one who had knocked him out . . . still, that was his own fault.

Mr. William and the man were taken off to a ward. I was stitched in Casualty. They said, giving me an injection against infection, "We'll keep you here for the night. There'll be a bit of reaction, a certain amount of shock."

"I wouldn't go home anyway," I said, "till Mr. William comes round."

Then we got down to business. I had a good strong cup of coffee, then set about letting my people and Mr. William's know. I said : "Please let me do my own phoning, it will be much less alarming for everybody."

They permitted it. I knew that neither my parents nor Mr. William's grandmother would be alarmed yet at our non-arrival. It had taken such a surprisingly short time, though while it was happening it had seemed an eternity. I rang Tattoo Bluff first. It would take them longer to get in. Mercifully, Jeff answered the phone.

As soon as he heard my voice he said : "Serena, you haven't had an accident, have you?"

"Not really, Jeff. We just went in for Mrs. Harrison's ring and surprised safe-breakers." I wasn't going to mention Mr. Rasmorton yet. It would hurt Mrs. Harrison too much. I explained as quickly as I could. If only I could have told them Mr. William had regained consciousness. But I said I thought he was not deeply concussed.

Then I got Mother. I was sorry it wasn't Father but didn't make the mistake of asking for him, which would have alarmed her. The fact that I was speaking to her vastly reassured her, anyway.

She said quickly, "We'll be down immediately, Serena. Patsy's home. She can stay with Debbie. I do hope Mr. William is round by the time we get there."

The police contented themselves with a very short

statement meanwhile. In some way they managed to lighten the situation for me, because it seemed to be so much in the line of their everyday work. They chaffed Father when he arrived, the more so, no doubt, because Dad had been at a meeting and still had his dog-collar on, about the fighting spirit of his daughter.

Then we all went up to the room Mr. William was in.

We hadn't been there five minutes when Mr. William began to stir, flickering his eyelashes and turning his head from side to side, which made him wince. He tried to open his eyes, didn't seem able to, then said very uncertainly, "Where's Serena? Is she hurt? Where's Serena?"

He drew a hand out from under the bedclothes and put it out gropingly. I took it firmly. "It's all right, Mr. William, I'm here. Not hurt at all. Take it easy. They're all rounded up."

At the other side of the bed the doctor nodded at me approvingly.

Mr. William got his eyes open, tried to focus them, not very successfully, and said : "Serena?" in the most imploring tone. I don't think he knew anyone else was in the room. Something was bothering him deeply.

I leaned forward as close as I could. "Yes, Mr. William?"

"Tell me . . . please . . . was it Rasmorton?"

I hesitated. Was he fit enough? Yet wasn't it better to tell the truth and get it over?

I said, gulping, "Yes, Mr. William, it was. He's at the police-station now."

He said, very feebly, "I thought so. Recognised his voice." Then, "Serena, let them know at the police-station . . . that his wife is . . . at the nursing-home. They mustn't shock her. And tell them that he used no violence. He wouldn't."

Then his eyes closed again.

I burst into tears. His first thought had been for Mrs. Rasmorton.

Bruno brought them all bar Bunty, who was home with Wilhelmina. They spent just a few moments with

Mr. William, who was able to recognise them and say he was all right, then they took us away so he could have peace and quiet.

They put me to bed in a private room too and let them have a further quarter of an hour with me.

Mrs. Harrison said: "They want me down at the police-station."

I said, "Mrs. Harrison, there's something I've got to tell you. It was an inside job. I'm afraid one of our employees arranged it. Mr. Rasmorton."

Her colour ebbed till I felt alarmed, and so did Bruno. He put an arm round her. "Now, honey, steady. You've got to take it. It does happen. I've known what it is to have a trusted hand betray my trust in him. Take it easy, Laura. *I'm* here. I'll see to things for you."

She leaned her head against him and in that moment I realised two things. One, how hard it is to be an employer. Two, how beautiful elderly love can be. Laura Durbridge ... Harrison ... had come to a tranquil harbour after many storms at sea.

She managed: "He's been with us fifteen years. He had such a good job. Always a bonus at Christmas. Now his future is in ruins. And his wife and children will suffer from the shame of it, the publicity."

Although it had touched me to tears when Mr. William's first thought had been for Rasmorton's wife, it had not surprised me. Because despite the way I resented Mr. William's free and easy ways with women, I knew that fundamentally he was exceptionally soft-hearted, but I'd thought his grandmother was of sterner stuff, more realistic, harsher. Now I realised that all I had heard of her earlier years from the staff just added up to a tough skin grown to protect the tender places.

A nurse appeared with some tablets and a tumbler of milk.

"She's had more than enough excitement for one night. Now she must go to sleep."

I said, fretfully, "But I wanted to keep going to look at Mr. William."

Kitty said, patting my hand, "It's all right, Serena. Jeff and I are going to stay with him. We've asked."

Naturally Mother and Father kissed me goodnight, but though I expected the warm-hearted Kitty to do so, I was most amazed when everyone, especially Mrs. Harrison, followed suit. She was last.

She bent over me and whispered, "Thank you for saving William from what could so easily have been a fatal blow, Serena."

I looked up at her and said, my lip trembling, "If only I had averted it completely!"

As I drifted off to sleep I realised something. Mr. William's first thought *hadn't* been for Rasmorton and his wife. It had been for *me*.

I thought of something else ... for a girl who had wanted so desperately to keep her business life and her private life separate, I hadn't succeeded very well. The whole clan had kissed me!

CHAPTER ELEVEN

THE next morning my arm was stiff and sore and I had bruises not suspected the night before. One, a large one, covered my left cheekbone. And I'd lost a tiny bit of eyebrow that gave me a comical look, I thought, like a cat that had been out on the tiles.

That, combined with a high-collared drill nightgown of hospital issue and an enormous utility dressing-gown of red serge, to say nothing of a pair of carpet slippers, made me a glamorous figure to visit Mr. William.

Only the fact that I still felt desperately worried about him made me visit him looking a guy like that.

But his smile from the bed made me feel as if I'd been dressed in a Paris model and diamonds. And he said to the nurse, "Thank you, Nurse, you can leave us alone now."

I hoped she wouldn't be offended. She was such a

sweet little thing, but as she vanished through the door she turned and gave me a saucy wink.

Mr. William saw it and said cheerfully, "She's got ideas about us. No wonder . . . man's secretary being escorted home by her boss . . . sneaking up to the office at midnight . . . oh, what a story!"

I went scarlet and clapped my cool hands to my hot cheeks.

I gulped and said: "We'll have to impress on the reporters that we were after your grandmother's ring."

He nodded. "I've thought of that. The police have been in. They found the ring. The thieves hadn't touched that though it was lying in full view. Too easily identifiable, I suppose. I asked the police to make mention of the fact that the ring we were after was safe and sound, in fact, to include it in the photos taken by the papers if they could. And I mentioned that we'd gone in before I took you home so that there would be some light on the subject."

I looked at him gratefully.

"They'll be back for a statement from you later, Serena. The nurse told me you were still flat out to it, so I said they were not to disturb you."

I was sitting in a chair close to his bed. He put up a hand and touched my purple cheek. "Serena, what can I say, how can I thank you? Most women would have stayed out of it. You'd done your part in getting help. I was terrified for you when you charged in. I—" He couldn't go on. He brought his hand down from my cheek and took my hand, and for a moment we looked deeply into each other's eyes, remembering that moment when it was just him and me against three.

He began to say something, but I said hurriedly, for I was afraid my eyes would give away all I felt for him, "I—I've always wondered how anyone could possibly get up enough feeling to actually leap into battle with the intention of really hurting someone. Now I know. When I saw you—against three—I really and truly saw red. And, Mr. William, I hate to remember it now, but I sort of went berserk, and for one horrible moment I actually—" I stopped, overcome by the

memory of it, and Mr. William's sherry-brown eyes
crinkled into laughter and he gave quite a shout and
said, "Oh, my Serene Miss Smith, I know exactly what
you were going to say! For a moment you actually
enjoyed laying about you!"

I said, hanging my head, "I don't think I'll tell anyone else. It—it's so unfeminine."

Mr. William said softly, "Not to me. I've always
admired the Amazons, you know. Listen, girl, you
couldn't have stayed out of it, could you? Tell me,
Serena, did you fight everyone's battles when you were
at school?"

I said lamely, "Well, I admit I was a tomboy. My
brother Douglas was a toughie, and he brought me up
to punch, not slap. Mr. William, I've not asked how
your head is yet. Though you look all right."

"I am. Just a bit of concussion. I've taken worse on
the Rugby field."

I said solemnly but nervously, "I think I'd better go
along and find out how that chap is that I—"

He chuckled again. "That you laid out cold? They
told me he came round much later than I did. But
also just concussion. But he's going to have a much
worse hangover than I've got, I'll swear, wondering
what's going to happen to him."

He sobered and his eyes looked bitter. "I got very
near the door. I heard one of them say. 'Pile up all
this stuff round the safe. We'll blow it up now and it's
bound to look like an outside job.' I heard another
voice say: 'Make dead sure the lock's gone, won't
you?' and I felt positively sick as I recognised
Rasmorton's voice.

"Two seconds after that Rasmorton began to come
out of the door and I could do nothing but charge
him. He rushed back inside and the other two sprang
at me. I'll hand this to Rasmorton, he recognised my
voice immediately, I suppose, and he didn't attack me
at all. He just fell back. They snarled at him to help,
but he wouldn't. It ought to help him. Lessen the
charges." He paused, then added in a strained voice,
"I liked the man. We've played golf together. I've even

been out to his house a couple of times. When I think of his wife—" he broke off. "I wonder if Bruno could help him get a fresh start over there. Though I daresay he wouldn't be a desirable migrant. But we'll have to do something to help him when he comes out. Serena, what on earth are you crying for? Don't you feel well? Here, I'll call a nurse. Wait—"

I scrubbed furiously at my eyes. I didn't seem to have a hanky. "No, I'm all right. It's just . . . well, you taking it like this."

Mr. William fished under his pillow and handed me a handkerchief. "It's not a really clean one, Serena, but better than nothing, I guess. Mop up and cheer up. I'm glad you cried . . . you wanted to be feminine, and there's nothing more feminine than tears. You are a goose, though. Look, I'm sick of being in bed, I'll get hold of a nurse and get my clothes. Let's both go home." He sprang out of bed, looking like a scarecrow in pyjamas much too short, and yanked a dressing-gown off the back of the door.

I clutched him. "Now, Mr. William, you mustn't! They'll still want you under observation."

At that auspicious moment an orderly arrived. "What's this? Rebellion against bed? Well, never mind, I'm taking you for a head X-ray. Just a precaution. Then if everything's all right, you can go home."

I was allowed to go home too. Mr. William's suit wasn't too bad, except for bloodstains, but I couldn't face going out into the prosaic morning light in a torn black lace frock. I'd feel like a gangster's moll. Finally I rang Father and he and Mother came down, and between us we decided Mr. William could stay up home for the day so that he'd be readily available for statements and questioning. Tattoo Bluff was too far out.

I was glad we were respectably dressed by the time the reporters and photographers arrived, though they liked the bloodstains, of course. Father was inclined to chuckle over the whole thing. We sat in the living-room, drinking coffee and re-living it.

Mr. William laughed reminiscently, "Never would

I have thought when I engaged Miss Serena Smith,
daughter of a Scots parson, with her mousy hairdo,
as smooth as if it had been gummed into place, and
dressed in a grey frock with white collar and cuffs, as
prim as a Quaker Maid of long ago, and as coldly
efficient as a punch-card machine, that some day she'd
be skirmishing around the office brandishing a T-stand
and yelling her head off, just like a Red Indian on the
warpath. Ever play golf, Serena? I reckon you'd have
a mighty stroke."

Dad said : "She played cricket. Probably felt it was
a case of a minute to play and six to win, so she slogged.
And while she may have struck you as prim and proper
that first day, Bill, let me tell you Serena has been in
the forefront of the battle from kindergarten days on.
I've always felt we ought to have called her
Boadicea."

Really! Families! Well, I'd wanted to be anything
but a glamour girl in my employer's eyes, hadn't I?

I found myself wondering how his Molly would have
acted under the same circumstances. I wasn't sure. No
doubt any woman, seeing the man she loved so out-
numbered, would have dashed into the fray. But—well,
Molly was beautiful, she was a superb horsewoman, tall,
and carried herself well, but, despite all that, to me she
appeared the clinging type.

Maybe that was what men liked best. For marriage,
anyway. Even Laura Harrison, the one-time matriarch,
was now sweetly dependent upon her Bruno.

Bruno rang. He said the shop was, of course, a hive
of conjecture and discussion. He suggested he brought
Laura up to the Manse for lunch. Mother and Father
were delighted. Oh, dear, we were getting in deep with
the Durbridges. In some ways it was a pity. I couldn't
deny to myself I was enjoying it, but it was going to
make it just that much harder, later, when they were
all back in the States, and I slowly but surely would
withdraw from personal contacts with my boss.

I thought of something. "Mr. William, the Christchurch papers will carry the story by this afternoon's
first edition. Molly will be worried. Would you like to

ring her from here? She might appreciate knowing how you are and speaking to you personally."

Bruno cut in. "She knows. Her father rang us. He saw the stop press in this morning's Times. He was going to ring her."

But I was surprised Mr. William didn't make a personal call. Perhaps his head was bothering him, what with the family talking ninety to the dozen, the police interviews, and so on, to say nothing of that wretched child, Debbie, rushing home for lunch and embracing Mr. William as one returned from the dead. She condescended to give me a slight peck and then continued to hang on his every word with sickening hero-worship.

"It would have made a smashing T.V. programme. You against three of them."

"Well, two," amended Mr. William, but he turned his head away a little. He didn't like being reminded of Rasmorton.

A thought struck Debbie. "Do you think they'll interview you on T.V.? Gosh, I hope they do. The kids'll turn green with envy. I had a great morning."

"I bet you did," I muttered. "And of course we won't be on T.V."

I was wrong. Like a stage cue the phone rang and it was for Mr. William from the T.V. News.

He came back laughing. "I'm afraid it's only too true, Serena. We're for it!"

"Now look what you've done," I said, quite unjustly, to Debbie. Then, "Debbie, have you gone mad? There's no need to throw your arms round Mr. William's neck."

"*I* call him Bill," said that demon child, "and you needn't look like that, Serena, he asked me to, long ago. And there *was* need. He said he was sure he could get *me* into that T.V. picture and if I was late he'd run me back to school and explain to the headmaster."

I said, laughing helplessly, "If only I had that T-stand to hand right now!"

Laura Harrison said fondly: "You sound just like William and Kitty used to. I love family life."

I gave up. Enough ordeals ahead without getting het up over my small sister's behaviour. T.V., indeed!

But Mr. William made it all much less of an ordeal though he said far too much about my part in the affair. He wangled Debbie into the picture for the news, much to her delight, and she even got a comment: "Miss Smith's small sister listens, enthralled, to the tale."

No wonder life seemed very flat and tame once the court proceedings were over and the shouting and the tumult died.

Bruno decided they'd stay on for a bit. "There's more goes on in the little old burgh than I thought possible," he said to me.

He and Father had taken a great fancy to each other. They even went off golfing together on Mondays and I heard them planning fishing.

Dad said: "You'll enjoy fishing for salmon in the Waitaki, Bruno. It's nearly ninety miles north, but a good road all the way. Plenty of trout nearer at hand too. Most of the rivers and Lake Mahinerangi up above Waipori, too."

I said, bewildered, "But, Dad, the season doesn't open till October. This is only July . . . mid-winter."

Bruno said: "Serena, we're only across the Pacific. I've decided Laura and I can spend a lot of time here. It's a tourist's paradise. Hunting, snow sports, hot springs . . . it's got everything. Besides, I don't intend to wrench Laura away from her family entirely. Except that our home must, of course, be in Texas. We'll go back in August probably, but we'll come back in November for the fishing, Angus."

Lucky, lucky Laura. But she deserved it.

Yes, we saw a lot of the family. Bruno, Laura, Kitty, Jeff, and, of course, the adorable Wilhelmina. She trotted round after Debbie like a little dog. Debbie loved that. And I must say she was sweet with Wilhelmina. So patient. My little sister was growing up.

She said one night, heaving a deep sigh, "I hope when I grow up I'll meet someone just like Mr. William, and marry him."

Even children fell for his charm.

But even though I could do nothing to prevent the way friendship was being fostered between Mr. William's family and mine, Mr. William took no advantage of it. He had accepted my refusal of him as an escort, finally.

Even the night the Tattoo Bluff family turned up at the West Hill Church, Mr. William wasn't there. I had an idea that when he had dropped Veronica or she had dropped him—whichever way it had gone— it must have cemented things between him and Molly. His girl-next-door.

Mother, of course, asked them all in to supper. I purposely did not ask where Mr. William was. But of course Debbie did.

Mrs. Harrison said: "He was meeting Molly at Momona. She was coming from Christchurch by the last plane. It seems funny to see William trotting round after her like this. When they were children together it was a different story. He'll do anything for her now. Molly was young enough to be a real embarrassment to her brothers and William.

"They used to try to sneak off without her on their tramping and fishing expeditions. Molly was just like a puppy to William ... forever at his heels. The boys were always telling Molly to find a girl friend. I once found William climbing down a dangerous and forbidden cliff path. I made him come back and demanded to know why. He said because just for once he wanted to go fishing without Molly tagging on and scaring the fish off because she couldn't stop talking for long. But now I reckon he'd dive off Tattoo Head if she wanted him to."

I laughed with the rest, but felt lower than low.

Debbie said, with great gusto, and hero-worshipping eyes, "He's the stuff heroes are made of, isn't he? The sort of man men would follow to their death in a war if he were their captain."

"For heaven's sake, Debbie," I said, hurriedly offering her a plate of jelly sponge, "have a wedge of this and come down to earth."

"Well," she said, hunting round the plate till she could find the biggest piece, "I bet you feel exactly the same about him, working for him as you do, only you're too old to show it."

She didn't mind a bit when they all laughed again. I suddenly found Father's eye on me, speculatively and shrewdly. I hastily averted mine.

The next morning some glorious samples of junior misses' suits came into the buying-room. One had a loose jacket with soft grey synthetic fur at neck and sleeves. It was exactly Debbie's size.

I bought it for her. I don't quite know why, unless something about the way she patently adored Mr. William did something for my own bottled-up feelings.

Mr. William said, "We get these samples at very low prices—through our London buyers. You can have it at cost price, Serena."

I shook my head. "No. Please, no. I don't want any special concessions. I like to be treated exactly like the rest of the staff. I don't see why a man's secretary should be treated differently."

Mr. William sighed. "I don't know that it was because you're my secretary. I thought it was a gesture of friendship. You're distressingly independent, Serena. And in certain circumstances I've done this sort of thing before. Mrs. Ledham in the mantles supports her family herself. I often put aside some of the samples and let her pick what she wants at cost price."

"That's rather different, Mr. William. That's meeting a certain situation. If I take concessions because of friendship, between our families, I could start trading on it."

He uttered a sound of pure scorn. "That's ridiculous! And as for friendship—" he broke off, and for the life of me I couldn't help asking :

"Yes, Mr. William? As for friendship—?"

He made an impatient gesture. "Oh, let it go. You wouldn't be interested, or would just come back at me—but one thing, Serena, you must allow. Your sense of fairness would see the rightness of this. You must permit me to replace that frock that got torn in the fracas."

I said slowly : "I don't like being recompensed for anything like that. It puts a commercial value on things that are above value. I'd rather—"

"Serena Smith! When Mrs. Jenkins ripped her skirt during those alterations to the furnishing department, I replaced it, didn't I? She suffered that damage in the course of my service. Well, so did you. For heaven's sake, girl, don't make such a fuss over small things. You make everything too personal."

I could do nothing but consent. He had the tailoring department make me one exactly the same and said with a twitch of his mouth, "Because I just dare not offer you a more expensive one out of stock, you termagant!"

Molly called in to see him one day. I gathered up my papers and prepared to depart, to melt unobtrusively into the outer office, as any well-trained secretary should when her employer's wife or fiancée calls. Well, they weren't engaged yet, but it was coming.

Molly stopped me. "Don't go, Serena. Or will our talking disturb you?"

I sat down again. Talk turned, later, on the burglary.

Molly said to Mr. William, "Of course, personally, Bill, I think you made things just too easy for Mr. Rasmorton."

He said nothing.

So she added : "Gran told me about you continuing a percentage of his salary to Mrs. Rasmorton. Fair enough, but when I heard you had also paid off his mortgage, I really raised my eyebrows."

I felt a wave of indignation rise in me, but could say nothing.

Mr. William said quietly, "There's such a thing as helping a man to rehabilitate himself. It's going to be hard enough for him when he comes out. I feel an accountant of his ability could set himself up in private practice. He'll have a certain amount of prejudice to overcome. He says he'd find it too embarrassing to come back here. He'd been plunging heavily on the

gee-gees, you know, and his tastes were expensive. Mad
on boats, spent too much on purchasing them. But I
did feel that if when he came out he didn't have too
big a load of debt round his neck, he'd find it easier
to make good."

"Okay, Bill," said Molly easily. "You've got a much
nicer nature than me, evidently. I couldn't go as far
as that. Your justice is more tempered with mercy,
seemingly." Suddenly she said slowly, "Bill, how was it
that you and Serena appeared so opportunely on the
scene that night? Or did the papers in Christchurch
get hold of the wrong time? It said midnight. Were
you working late, and was it much earlier?"

"No, of course not. Had we been working late there'd
have been others there too. It's never been a practice of
mine to work late with just one woman. No employer
would—he'd be mad if he did. And in that case there'd
have been lights on, therefore no attempt. Didn't the
Christchurch papers say why we came in?—I was
taking Serena home after the family dinner. We put
it on for Gran. Had you been home you'd have been
there.

"Gran suddenly missed her ring, that opal one that
belonged to her mother, and she wouldn't have slept
had she not known it was safe and sound." He hesitated
and added, "There were a few louts in the street, so I
didn't want Serena to wait in the car, to say nothing
of the fact that she'd be useful looking for the ring if it
hadn't been where Gran said it probably would be."

Molly seemed satisfied. "Oh, was that how it was?
Sheer curiosity on my part, Bill. Good job you did
come in. The papers up there simply said the three men
were disturbed by Mr. William Durbridge and his
secretary. You know these things tease your mind. I
meant to ask you before."

But the whole thing made me vastly uncomfortable.
Mr. William went downstairs with her, saying some
new furs had arrived, that he had an idea her mother
wanted one for a wedding, and he'd give Molly some
on approval.

I'd told myself earlier that it would be all for the

best if he did marry Molly, that I'd make myself happy
in the thought that he was happy. And to hope, after
he was married, that never again would he play round
with three girls at once.

All of a sudden I wasn't so sure. Would Molly make
him happy? She was a lovely girl in many ways, but
would she—quite—understand his nature? His contra-
dictory nature. It seemed as if she had forgiven the
affair of Veronica and I hoped she'd never know he
had tried to make love to me, but if a wife didn't understand—and appreciate—the heart-warming generosity
of a man in a situation like this, helping the man who
had betrayed his friendship, would there be between
them perfect accord? Would they reach the heights
together? As Mother and Father did.

Sometimes when some knotty problem in church
work arose, I'd seen, across a crowded room, a certain
look from Father to Mother. An unspoken question
answered only by a trustful, confident look from her.
And Father would be strengthened to act as he must
act even if at times it went against the grain, for Father
was essentially a peaceful man, but not a peace-at-any-
price one.

But Molly, this morning, had made Mr. William
appear, in front of a member of his staff, me, a little
too quixotic. And it had jarred on me.

CHAPTER TWELVE

I KNEW it was not imagination that after that Mr.
William seemed very absent-minded for him. Not dull,
he could never be that, he was too dynamic, but he was
certainly preoccupied.

I felt he forced himself to be interested and enthusiastic about shop matters. We were right in the thick of
the winter now ... sometimes Mount Flagstaff and
Mount Cargill were covered in snow and then we'd

get a succession of sharp frosts. The hill roads would be icy traps and the Corporation trucks would be out early throwing gravel screening on.

As an Aucklander, I naturally longed for a really spectacular fall of snow. It would be such fun. Father had made Debbie a toboggan, hoping for it. Our street was terrifically steep and I'd heard tales of people actually tobogganing down it. I often looked up at the grey, leaden sky from the office windows and said hopefully, "Are we in for a heavy fall, Mr. William?" It used to make him laugh.

He said once, "I think it must be three years since we had a fall like that. The shop had to do without me for three days. I hate driving in chains and nobody is indispensable, anyway. And though it's not so bad coming in to Dunedin now we have the motorway, it's still high enough and there are usually cars stranded everywhere."

So I stopped hoping for snow. I couldn't bear the thought of the office without Mr. William.

September came in and with it the promise of spring. Crocuses popped up in the bare beds in the Octagon, green spears thrust up in our garden, and the prunus began to show a diaphanous hint of blossom. The forsythia decked itself in living gold and put the winter jessamine twigs in the shade.

I found violets on my office desk. Yes, Mr. William's, but they didn't mean a thing. They were on the outer desks too. But I buried my face in their sweetness and said : "Most florist's violets are large but scentless. These are smaller and sweeter."

He said, quite casually, as he went out of the door, "Oh, those are from home. We have a very sheltered bed of them."

Had he picked them? Or would it be Kitty or Bunty?

Kitty and Jeff were staying on instead of going back to Christchurch. Mrs. Ralston was so enjoying her unexpected holiday in New Zealand she wanted to see it all before going back home and was at present up in the thermal area in the North Island. Bruno had now booked flights for October. But he would come back, he said, for the novelty of celebrating Christmas in summertime.

I said to Mr. William once, noticing fine lines beneath his eyes I'd not seen before, and a slightly more angular look to his jaw, "Mr. William, are you feeling well?"

He didn't seem surprised, that was what worried me afterwards, when I thought about it. He simply said, "I'm quite well, Miss Smith. Why?"

"I thought you seemed a little thinner ... and quieter."

Instantly his face tightened a little and for the first time in our association I felt I was the one who had trespassed a little, personally. A most uncomfortable feeling. Perhaps because it underlined for me that now he was the one who preferred us to be merely business associates.

Then he said, quite lightly, "Oh, I expect I lost a bit of weight over the Rasmorton business. And we're lambing. In many ways it's been an eventful year ... Jeff getting hurt, Gran getting wed."

I wanted to suggest he took a spring holiday instead of a January summer one; I wanted to beg him to ease up at the shop, most of all I wanted to ask him had it by any chance made trouble between him and Molly, the fact that we came up here together, alone, so late at night. Did she resent the fact that it was so publicised? But I didn't dare ask.

I was almost sure it had to do with Molly, this quietness and heaviness of spirit in someone who was by nature exuberant, brimming over with fun. It could be, of course, since Molly's comments on Rasmorton indicated she wasn't the easily forgiving kind, that she still resented the way he had run Veronica Boleyn round.

Pity if she couldn't forgive and forget it. After all, it was up to her to keep him so interested that his glance didn't stray. The irony of my changed attitude towards him struck me with wry humour. Once I'd thought him a poor husband risk. Now I only longed for the chance. But he was no longer interested in me.

Then came the day when I was waiting in the advertising clerk's office. Mr. William had sent me for some information and they were digging it out of some ancient files for me. His grandmother hadn't come in with him that morning. She didn't always now, Bruno wouldn't let her. He couldn't stand being without her all day.

I sat down at one of the high desks that held the newspaper folders. Every paper was scanned every day, not only for our own advertisements but for our rivals. Our own were cut out, pasted in scrapbooks, their measurements noted, ready for checking against the accounts as they came in. I began turning over the morning paper which I never had time to read at home till after dinner.

I read idly, little snippets of news. Suddenly a name in the engagement column leapt up at me. I stared at it blankly.

Molly's name.

I read it again, disbelievingly. Oddly, the one thing that seemed to register was the fact that her baptismal name really was Molly, not Mary.

I read it still once again. "Mr. and Mrs. Hubert Raeburn, of Moko Point, Blueskin Bay, have much pleasure in announcing the engagement of their only daughter, Molly Valentine, to Richard, third son of Mr. and Mrs. Andrew Farrington, Cashmere Hills, Christchurch."

I suddenly realised one of the copywriters had spoken to me twice. I gathered my wits together, took the profferred notes, then said, "May I borrow this paper, Miss Fearon? I—there's something in it I think Mr. William would be—er—interested to see. I'll return it later."

Anne Fearon said, "Of course. Actually, we've finished with it—as you can see from its mutilated condition. Don't bother to return it. They go into the waste bin every night after clipping. Just throw it out. It's only an hour to closing time."

I went very slowly up the stairs, through the outer office and into ours that was sandwiched between that and the inner sanctum that Mr. William and his grand-mother used for private interviews.

I looked at Mr. William's bent brown head as he wrestled with some sales analysis and laid down the notes he had wanted beside him.

He muttered perfunctorily "Thank you, Miss Smith," and I returned to my own desk.

I sat there with the paper under my hand. What had happened? Was this the reason for Mr. William's lost weight, his apathy? She was engaged to a Christchurch man. Had she been caught on the rebound...? She hadn't, I was almost sure, rung him from Christchurch when that news was in the paper. Had she, remembering Veronica, seen in our escapade, quite wrongly, further proof that he was given to infatuations? Any girl could have misgivings over a thing like that.

I was sure it dated from there. I'd thought at the time that had she loved Mr. William as I loved him, she'd have dashed home to reassure herself he was all right.

Yes, this coolness between them dated back to that. She'd read in that paper that Mr. William and I had been alone in that office at midnight. And I was that arch-suspect...a blonde. I felt slightly sick. Mr. William was fretting, so he did love her. That episode of ours had tied up in Molly's mind with the hurt she had suffered when he had been taking Veronica out. Disillusioned, torn by doubts of him, she'd been caught on the rebound by someone else. And now, too late, he knew where his affections lay. Even though, after she had come back from Christchurch, it had been explained to her, she still mustn't have believed him—us. Anyway, by then she was probably too deeply in with the other chap.

Mr. William's voice broke into my bewildered and dismayed reflections.

"Miss Smith, what's the matter? You've gone into a trance. I do want those letters off by five-thirty, you know." Then, quickly, "Serena, what is it? You look as if you've had a bit of a shock. What is it?"

I moistened my lips, said, "Yes, yes, there is something wrong. I—Mr. William, just bear with me. This will seem far too personal, but I feel I ought to tell you—" I came to a full stop.

His eyes had narrowed. "Of course I'll bear with you. Take a deep breath and start again. Who's been upsetting you?"

"Oh, it's not a staff matter. It's personal," I said. "Mr. William, *did* you and Molly have a quarrel over me being up here with you that night?"

He looked completely blank. "Quarrel? Over *you*? Why the devil should we?"

I crimsoned hotly. "I know it sounds presumptuous. Only she did ask about it here. And you've been so preoccupied and you've lost weight. I know you've fretted. But—well, you haven't seemed particularly upset today, so you can't have seen it yet . . . she ought to have prepared you, it isn't fair to let you read it in the paper. Mr. William, have you read this morning's paper yet, all of it?"

I stood up, the paper in my hand, and came towards his desk.

He was staring up at me. "Well, I read the leader and the main news—and of course the ads—but why?"

I said faintly, "Then you wouldn't have read the engagement columns?"

This time he really boggled. "No, I never do. Men don't, I think. But what—"

I thrust the paper at him. "It's in here, I'm afraid, Mr. William . . . Molly's engagement to a man in Christchurch."

He grabbed it off me, said in a perfectly normal tone, "Oh, have they actually announced it?"

It was too much for me. I fell back against the back of my desk.

"Mr. William," I spluttered, "you know? You knew? And you don't—you don't—"

He put his head on one side and said: "Serena Smith! If you don't stop stuttering and stammering I'll shake you good and proper. I don't *what*?"

I gulped. It had to be said. "You don't—don't *mind*?"

I've never heard anyone sound so exasperated. He said : "*Mind*? Why the hell should I mind? I'd much rather this chap than the one who couldn't make up his mind which girl he wanted. Serena Smith, what nonsense is this?"

I took a deep breath. My mind was whirling. I said firmly, "Mr. William, weren't you in love with Molly?"

Then he really did stare. He said slowly : "How could I be? I wouldn't marry my cousin, wouldn't fall in love with my cousin . . . a double cousin at that. Her father is Mother's brother, her mother is Father's sister . . . Gran's daughter, you crazy idiot !"

Crazy idiot . . . crazy idiot . . . I shall always think those two words the most beautiful in the English language. My heart was beating so fast it threatened to suffocate me. Stars were bursting all about me.

I managed : "Your *cousin* ! But you never said . . . nobody said . . . oh, *why* didn't they when they introduced me?" Then something hit me . . . the overheard telephone conversation.

I said, looking him straight in the eye, "Mr. William, you have something to explain. You'll think me an eavesdropper, but I couldn't help it. You remember that morning after we got back from taking Wilhelmina up to Christchurch? You told me I was not to come to work early. I got there at the usual time and walked in to hear you on the phone. You were telling Molly that she was a goose, that she mustn't develop an inferiority complex and think of herself just as the girl-next-door. You said your infatuation for Veronica was only a flash-in-the-pan, that it didn't mean a thing. That *she* wasn't the sort of girl a chap wanted to marry. You *did*, Mr. William. There *must* have been something between you. Don't you understand? I couldn't bear to read of her engagement in the papers. I knew I had to break it to you myself . . . but now I don't know what to believe, what to think, what—"

But Mr. William had me by the shoulders now and his fingers were biting into my flesh. I could feel the nails. He shook me, but there was a light in his eyes I'd never seen before, a light that was only dawning, and I knew it would be reflected in my eyes too...

He said: (shake) "Serena, they say listeners never hear any good of themselves... *they also hear only part.* I remember that conversation... of course I can't remember it word for word... but get this into your head" (shake) "that I was not talking about *my* infatuation for Veronica. I was talking about the other chap who fell for Veronica and dropped Molly. The chap my cousin was in love with, Vincent Shaw.

"Molly was broken-hearted. Veronica is a money-grabber... we got the idea, Molly and I, that if I rushed Veronica, she would drop Vince, and he would realise just what she is. That's exactly what did happen. I took her out to every place I knew Molly was going to. It sounds hard on Veronica, but it didn't hurt her—not in the emotions—nothing could, so for goodness' sake, don't lecture me on that. I couldn't stand it." (Shake.)

"She dropped Vince like a hot potato—*he's* only a wage-earner. I felt like Sir Galahad, no end puffed up about myself. Then blow me down if Molly didn't change her mind! Women, really!" (shake) "Molly was delighted when Vince swung back to her, began taking her out again. I kept on dating Veronica... well, her rapture lasted about a week. You see, during the time I was rushing Veronica Molly had gone up to some Christchurch relatives of ours and had met Richard, but at that stage she wouldn't even trust her own feelings. So she came back home, and found out. Richard's a much finer chap. I'm much happier about it. Vince is a born flirt, I doubt if he'll ever change. But" (shake) "I once asked you if you wanted Veronica explained and you didn't. You were most withering, Miss Serena Smith!"

(Shake, shake, shake.)

He broke off and peered into my face. "Serena, you've got to tell me and tell me true. You heard me saying those things—those dreadfully ambiguous things the morning after our Christchurch weekend. That

terrifically frustrating weekend when first of all Gran
came back out of the blue and then I couldn't even
get you to myself on the plane. You know what I'm
leading up to, Serena . . . it was the Monday after that
night . . . you know which one I mean now" (shake)
"so don't turn your face away, girl, meet my eyes!
The Monday after the night we shared . . . oh, blast,
what a row from that office, what the devil *is* going
on out there? Here, where's that engaged notice? Oh,
I think it's in the Sanctum."

He released me so abruptly I fell back against my
desk and had to steady myself with both hands.

As he reached the inner door it flew open and there,
framed in the opening, was his grandmother!

Mr. William and I looked completely horrified, and
I, at least, embarrassed.

"Gran!" he roared. "How did you get in there? I
didn't even know you were in town! Of all the things
to—"

She silenced him with an imperial hand. "William,
now you just listen to me. I came in when you were out
of the office. I just didn't dare stop you when you
seemed to be in full flow . . . and if ever explanations
seemed to be needed, this was the time. I was just
terrified I'd sneeze or something or that someone from
the other office would rush in, or the phone ring. It's
a mercy it hasn't.

"How any two people could get their lines crossed the
way you two have is beyond my ken, when you're
obviously destined for each other! Why do you think
Bruno and I keep postponing returning to Texas, if
not for the fact we'd like to give you our blessing
personally? I thought you were being awfully slow,
William."

Mr. William gave her an incredulous look. So did I.
Then for a moment we all three gazed at each other
blankly because no one knew exactly how to go on from
here. Then another burst of conversation from the other
office galvanised us into action. Or at least it affected
Mr. William and his grandmother that way.

He said, on a great burst of laughter, "Right, Gran,

out you go ... and bar the door. This is *really* a case
of two's company, three's a crowd," just as she said,
"I'll get that engaged sign, it's in here," and she disappeared into the Sanctum, reappeared with it, waving
it like a banner, and said, laughing, "Engaged in more
ways than one," and rushed across the office, only to
have that door flung open in her face and Mr. Jennings
to appear on the heels of a most perfunctory knock.

We all blinked. He was too full of what he had to
say to notice anything strange about any of us. He
said : "Mr. William, I'm sorry, but a stupid woman in
the showroom absolutely demands to see the proprietor.
She's completely in the wrong. She bought a blouse off
Miss Denham last week, is trying to exchange it now
on the grounds of it being too small, but it's obviously
been worn, though she's pressed it and re-attached the
ticket. Now she's trying to say Miss Denham gave her
the wrong size. I told her it was my job to handle this,
but she was adamant."

Mr. William said, in a tone Mr. Jennings had never
heard before, "Just lead me to her, I'll choke her with
my bare hands !"

But his grandmother cut in, "Wants to see the proprietor, does she? Well, that's still me. Where is she?
Mr. William is not to be disturbed—he's in the middle
of proposing to Miss Smith. Out you go !" And she
swept the startled Mr. Jennings out in front of her and
we could just imagine the sensation in the outer office
(they must have heard every word) as she slammed
the door behind her and announced to them all clearly :
"Mr. William is not to be interrupted for anything short
of fire !" And (presumably) hung the notice on the door.

I had the queerest feeling. *Was* it a proposal? How
absolutely ghastly for any man if he hadn't meant quite
that ... but his grandmamma had taken the situation
clean out of his hands. Then I lifted my head and
looked at Mr. William and all doubts fled.

He was leaning back against the door as if to bar it
to all comers. His hand was feeling for the key behind
him and I heard it click as it went home. His eyes met
mine.

He crossed the room towards me, halted a couple of paces away and said, smiling, "And what a proposal! I suggest we ratify the whole thing tonight, Miss Smith, under a moon. Might I suggest Lake Waihola?" He laughed. "There's so much to explain. Serena, how on earth was I to guess you thought I was in love with my darling, dilly cousin Molly? Or to realise you didn't know she *was* my cousin. But you must have heard her calling Fran Gran."

"Yes . . . but I thought you'd always known each other . . . with living next-door. I mean we always called our next-door neighbour in Paihia Auntie Lucy." That reminded me of something. "And you *did* say, on the phone that morning, she mustn't think she was only the girl-next-door. What else was I to think?"

"Vince's folk farm next door to Molly's folk. On the other side. Serena, was that why you wouldn't go with me to that play? Why you wouldn't go to watch the moon rise? Why you lied and said Lance was taking you out?"

I nodded. "I thought you were two-timing. In fact, three-timing. Me, Molly, Veronica. With Molly the likely candidate for the marriage stakes."

He added softly, still smiling, so that he had creases in his cheeks, "And tell me, Serena, was that the reason why, at Lake Waihola, you wouldn't allow yourself to respond? Or am I vain in thinking that your only reason?"

This time my eyes met his in the most candid look we'd shared for weeks, a look that held nothing back, and I said, clearly and distinctly, "There's only one way of finding out . . . I suggest you try again!"

He closed the gap between us, his arms came round me, strained me to him hungrily. There weren't any bulrushes between us, no misunderstandings.

I said, quite strongly, seeing I felt as if I hadn't a bone left in my body, "The *only* reason . . . oh, if only you knew what it cost me *not* to respond . . . Oh, Mr. William, Mr. William, Mr. William!"

And then I couldn't say anything more for a long, long time.

But you have to draw breath some time.

Then he said, laughing in a queer, exultant sort of way, "Really, can this be my *Serene* Miss Smith? You really are something when you let yourself go! Oh, but I like you this way, my girl. And listen, my darling idiot, you can't go on calling me Mr. William for the rest of your life. You sound like something out of a Victorian novel. It's Bill, darling."

I said slowly, "I'm going to find it hard. I've got so used to it. But I'll have to try."

"Well, you'd better get some practice in pronto. None of your long engagements for me. Let's get Bruno and Gran to postpone their flights just a little longer. You see, Kitty and Jeff are here too, and Mrs. Ralston. Mum and Dad can fly home. They're in Spain. You'd better see the bridal department tomorrow about your wedding gown. And none of your fierce independence about Durbridge's paying for it. Think of the advert we'll get. We'll make it something out of this world. And never will there have been a prettier bride.

"Oh. my love, those letters! Look, Serena, you aren't to do them. Think of the mistakes you'd make. I'll get Miss Harris in. I must phone first, though."

Bemused, I saw him reaching for the phone. I heard him say: "Mr. Smith? Oh, it's Bill Durbridge here. There's a couple coming up to see you about getting married. Hope you're going to be free. You are? Oh, good ... it's us. Serena and me. What? You aren't surprised? Well, let me tell you *I* am. We've got our difficulties sorted out at last. Complete confusion from beginning to end. She thought, the silly rabbit, that I was going to marry Molly. Molly's my cousin. Well, it's too long a story for the phone. We'll be home for dinner, but we may be a little late. My proposal got all mixed up with an irate customer. Right now I've got to go down and rescue my granny from her. Except that she's so pleased about our engagement that she'll probably have given the woman half a dozen blouses by now. What a life! And Serena is trying to get some mail finished. So long."

I was staring at him. "It sounded as if you'd already talked things over with my papa."

Mr. William grinned. "I did. He asked me one day when I ran into him in town if you and I had quarrelled. I said no, but evidently you weren't interested in me. I told him I thought you were only interested in professional men, not drapers and farmers ... no, Serena, hold it, no temper! You can't possibly quarrel with me when we've just got engaged. Your father reacted just the same. Trounced me for daring to think it, said if his daughter was as intellectually snobbish as that, he'd spank her! So I decided I'd rushed you too much, asking you out as soon as you began working for me. I was waiting, hoping you'd get fond of me by degrees. And I've never been a patient man.

"Now, Serena, we've got all night tonight ... at Lake Waihola, to sort things out. If we want to. I can think of better things to do. Get Miss Harris to help you with those thrice-accursed letters—after we've faced the office staff together and received their felicitations. We'll have dinner at your place, talk things over with your parents—and, of course, the adorable Deborah. That's all I'm marrying you for, really, to have her as my sister. I bet she knows what colour she wants for her bridesmaid's frock, to say nothing of what Patsy should choose, long before we've reached the pudding stage. And then it *is* going to be Lake Waihola, isn't it, Miss Smith?"

"Yes, Mr. William," I said, as he unlocked the door and drew me forward.

CHAPTER THIRTEEN

HE had his way about it all. I was quite content to have it so.

It was a late October wedding, the month when in Otago the golds of the daffodils and jonquils give place to the purples and pinks of lilac and hawthorn.

We had been married at nine in the morning at our lovely church of St. Adrian's on West Hill. Father had conducted the wedding; Douglas had given me away. Durbridge's had styled the gowns and catered for the wedding feast. Feast it was, for apart from friends and relations, Mr. William had invited the entire staff. But Bunty had made the wedding cake and Hayley had iced it.

But now that was all of fourteen hours behind us. Fourteen since I had said, "I, Serena, take thee, William . . ." and he had whispered, "Last time for this William business, my girl."

It had been an early wedding because we had wanted to reach here tonight. "Here" was Lake Wakatipu, meaning the Trough-of-the-Goblin. Mr. William had brought me to one of the loneliest, loveliest spots in New Zealand.

We'd come up the Central Otago Highway, past acres of orchards just beginning to set fruit, bringing far more wealth than ever those same rugged contours had yielded in the gold-rush days. Through gorge and pass we had come to the little town of Queenstown, looked down on by the Remarkables, those jagged peaks, still crested by snow.

We had left the car there. A launch had been waiting to take us to the opposite shore, where no roads reached.

It had been brilliantly, unbelievably blue then, reflecting the snowy ranges in its still waters.

But now the lake was reflecting stars and a moon-track made a golden pathway across the fathomless waters. The bay was all ours, the world was all ours. There was just one little cottage here, ours for the honeymoon. Our only means of access was a private launch. The one that had brought us over had returned.

There was no electricity, no phone, only us.

We walked amongst the willows and birches by the water's edge, talking of the past, of the glorious present, of our fair future. A future that for my husband would not hold the turmoil and pressure of business life but would be lived on the land, at Tattoo Bluff, the life he had always craved.

Granny had seen to that. Durbridge's was to become a company, with Mr. Jennings as manager holding a few shares.

Hand in hand we came up the track from the bay. A morepork, our native owl, hooted from the dark hills towering above us, hills we would explore, sweet with native bush, the haunt of *tuis* and bellbirds.

And there before us was the little cottage. We had lit the lamp to guide us home before we set out on our ramble, the last ramble of my girlhood . . . by tomorrow I would have entered into a woman's heritage.

The light glowed goldenly, spilling out a welcome across the scented flowers of the old, neglected garden.

My husband stopped, said, "Serena, do you remember that night . . . that *first* night at Waihola? That poem I quoted that you said—you wretch—was *nice*?"

I nodded. The lines of that poem were graven on my heart for all time, but I wanted to hear his voice say them again, when there was no misunderstanding between us any more.

He said slowly:

"Houses seem so happy towards the close of day,
    Firelight-filled and lamplit, their worries put away.
    Easy to imagine lovely things behind
    Amber-tinted curtain and shadow-haunted blind."

I turned and clung to him in a tide of feeling that overwhelmed me.

He said, his chin on my head, "We're done with imagining now, Serena, my love. Let's go in."

And what do you think I said?

I said : "Yes, Mr. William."